D0437673

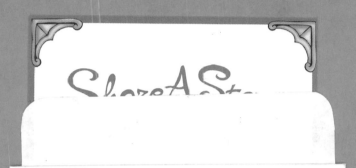

THE WIZARD TEST

HILARI BELL

THE
WIZARD
TEST

An Imprint of HarperCollins*Publishers*

Eos is an imprint of HarperCollins Publishers.

The Wizard Test

Printed in the United States of America.
For information address HarperCollins Children's Books,
a division of HarperCollins Publishers,
1350 Avenue of the Americas, New York, NY 10019.
www.harpereos.com

Library of Congress Cataloging-in-Publication Data
Bell, Hilari.
The wizard test / Hilari Bell.— 1st U.S. ed.
p. cm.
Summary: Fourteen-year-old Dayven is devastated when he learns he has wizard powers,
since wizards are considered to be disloyal deceivers who believe in nothing, until he under-
goes wizard training and discovers a new way of looking at the world that will change his
values, friendships, and future.
ISBN 0-06-059940-5 — ISBN 0-06-059941-3 (lib. bdg.)
[1. Wizards—Fiction. 2. Perception—Fiction. 3. Friendship—Fiction. 4. Fantasy.]
I. Title.
PZ7.B38894Wi 2004
[Fic]—dc22   2004002305

Typography by Larissa Lawrynenko
1 2 3 4 5 6 7 8 9 10

First Edition

For Kara Anne Schreiber—
fellow writer and good friend

THE WIZARD TEST

CHAPTER ONE

"**W**IZARD BORN!"

Dayven reached for his sword hilt as he spun in search of the speaker. Early in the morning the courtyard was crowded— not only with Watcherlads like Dayven, who'd come for a little extra sword practice, but also with adult Guardians, who were there to increase their skills with sword and lance. Someone had put a lot of effort into that hissing whisper, to make it audible over the clang of metal on metal . . . but who?

Was it Marret, who was so busily examining his practice blade for nicks? Or perhaps Benen, who was gathering up discarded shields for the Sword Master. Or maybe it was Thell, or Ryn, or . . . Dayven's shoulders sagged. It could have been any of them.

1

"Ignore it," his cousin Soren advised coolly, laying a hand on Dayven's shoulder. But his eyes also searched the crowd for the source of the whispers. Whispers that had been dogging Dayven for months, ever since the other Watcherlads realized that his fourteenth birthday was approaching.

"No," said Dayven. He raised his voice. "I want the stinking coward to show himself! Whatever my grandmother may have been, at least I have the courage to face my opponents, not whisper behind their backs like . . . like a wizard."

The whisper, though it had reached both Dayven and Soren, hadn't been loud enough to attract adult attention. Dayven's challenge rang through the yard, leaving silence in its wake, and several of the Guardians turned to stare. "He turns fourteen today," one of them murmured.

There was nothing but sympathy in the Guardian's voice, but Dayven's heart was too raw for him to be reasonable. His hand clenched on his sword hilt and he stepped forward, as Soren's grip on his shoulder tightened. But before he committed the insanity of challenging a full Guardian, another voice intervened. "What goes on here?"

Dayven froze under Lore Master Senna's stern gaze. "Nothing, sir."

The old Lore Master limped forward. He had been a Guardian himself, before a Cenzar blade had cut his leg so badly that even wizard healing hadn't been able to mend it completely. It was rumored that he hated the wizards for that, though he had never showed that hatred to the Watcherlads, when he taught them the history of the Tharn and the Guardians' creed.

The Lore Master turned to the waiting crowd. "If nothing is happening, then I suggest you go about your business. Surely you have better ways to serve the Lordowner than by gawking at . . . nothing."

The irony in his well-trained voice scattered the Watcherlads like chaff in a brisk breeze. He turned back to Dayven.

"Go. It will soon be resolved, and this trouble will end." The words were kind, but the Lore Master's eyes were cool and assessing—as they had always been when they looked at Dayven.

"Yes, sir. Thank you, sir," said Soren, pulling on Dayven's arm.

Dayven managed a respectful nod before his cousin dragged him away.

"Well, that should keep them quiet for the rest of the day," said Soren, as they turned their swords in to the armorer. "And by dinnertime it will never be a problem again."

"He said 'resolved,'" said Dayven bitterly as they headed up the spiraling stone stair to the room they shared. "He didn't say how."

"Resolved in your favor," said Soren confidently. "That's what he meant, of course."

Dayven thought that bards were more careful with words than that—especially the bard who was the official keeper of the history of the Tharn—but he said nothing.

Unfortunately, his cousin had always been able to read his silences. "Why don't you like him?" Soren asked.

"He watches me," said Dayven.

"He keeps an eye on all of us," said his cousin. "He's one of our instructors. It's part of his job."

"I know," said Dayven. It was true, too. But perceptive as Soren was, he didn't see that while Lore Master Senna observed all the boys he taught, noting the strengths and flaws in their characters, it was only Dayven that he watched for signs of magic. And never more so than he had in these last few months, as

Dayven approached his fourteenth birthday. This afternoon, while Soren and the others were working at the tasks the Lordowner's steward would set them, Dayven would be going to take the wizard test.

Dayven stared at the rusty gate separating the wizards' compound from the rest of the Town-within-the-Walls.

His stomach twisted and he took a deep breath. Despite the rumors that abounded among the common folk, even Lore Master Senna admitted that magic wasn't hereditary. And besides, Soren had taken the test last year, when he'd turned fourteen. If Soren hadn't inherited their grandmother's power, surely Dayven hadn't either. He was certain he couldn't work magic. Almost certain. The ability was rare. Every Tharn had to take this test, some time in their fourteenth year, and in Dayven's whole memory only one other Watcherlad had shown the gift—a clumsy, awkward boy who could never have been a Guardian. Dayven heard that there were some people who actually wanted to be wizards, but not boys who had a chance to become Guardians. Not Dayven

He pushed the gate open and approached the great stone tower where the wizards worked. Green scents from the neat herb garden filled the air. Wizards needed herbs for the medicines they made. So did the respectable surgeons, but they practiced no magic and were part of a man's destiny, not an intrusion, a thwarting of fate.

And yet, the sorcerer's medicines worked better—that was why they were tolerated. It was a rare man who, injured, ill, in pain, would put his true destiny above his life . . . as Dayven's mother had.

She had died when he was only nine years old, refusing the wizard's healing that might have saved her, in her shame for what her own mother had done. Dayven had begged her . . .

His jaw clenched, and he thrust the memory away.

The tower loomed over him. It was actually part of the great wall that surrounded the town. The wizards had been given the largest tower by Lord Gant, over a hundred years ago. Officially, it was because they needed a large space for their libraries and alchemical workshops. But most people believed they had been granted that tower because it was as far from the palace as you could get and still remain within the wall.

Dayven stood before the heavy door, trying to gather courage. Sly faces peered from between the leafy vines carved on its panels; the knocker was in the form

of a serpent, biting its own tail. Dayven sympathized—
the last few months had left him with a profound desire
to bite something. But that would soon be over. He
griped the snake's head and thumped the planks twice.

The door swung open. "Dayven, son of Bran?" The
doorkeeper squinted, gazing from the dimness of the
entry into the bright yard.

Dayven relaxed slightly. He had been afraid the
doorkeeper would address him as the grandson of
Adina. But that was foolish. He had always used his
father's name, and no taint of wizardry or dishonor had
ever touched his father's family. The wizards probably
had no idea who his maternal grandmother was. He
studied the doorkeeper's drab gray robe with faint con-
tempt. Wizards were almost always shabby.

The doorkeeper led him up a flight of spiral stairs,
their footsteps echoing on the worn stone. Dayven
guessed they were several floors up when the man
stopped.

"Wait here." The doorkeeper passed through a thick-
planked door, leaving Dayven alone on the landing.

Gazing at the dark wood, Dayven felt a stab of fear.
It was *not* hereditary, he told himself fiercely. He
wouldn't be so nervous if he knew more about the test,
but the wizards' secrets were closely guarded. He had

7

never been injured badly enough to need wizard's healing, and he'd promised his mother he would never have anything to do with magic, so he'd never tried to watch what the wizards did. Now he wished he had.

The temptation to ask Soren about the test had been almost overwhelming, but Soren would never break a vow of silence and Dayven couldn't risk losing his cousin's respect. It sometimes seemed to Dayven that Soren was the person he'd always wanted to be. There were rumors that Soren might win the sword and whistle of a Guardian this year, young as he was. Soren could have chosen anyone to be his best friend, for all the Watcherlads liked him, and it still seemed odd to Dayven that his cousin had befriended him. He might have suspected that Soren had done so out of pity, except that Soren was always honest, even about friendship. Besides, Dayven had his own friends among the boys who served the Lordowner—or at least, he'd had friends until his birthday approached and the whispers started. He jumped as the door swung open.

"We're ready for you." The shabby wizard held the door for him. Dayven started into the room and froze, staring.

It was a sorcerer's lair, right out of every scary story he'd ever heard. The table and benches were cluttered

with strange tools, bottles of colored liquids and pow-
ders, and a basket of what looked like dried snake skins.
Dayven wasn't familiar with many of the objects, but
the human skull, sitting casually on a pile of books, was
all too recognizable. It was said that keeping a dead
man's bones would attract his ghost; evidently wizards
didn't worry about that.

Potted plants sat on the table, and hanging bundles
of herbs swayed in the draft from the open door. A
small brown owl perched among the rafters. Dayven
was wondering why anyone would put a stuffed owl up
there when it blinked at him.

The only light came from a fat candle on the table
and a dimly glowing brazier on the floor. The corners of
the room were lost in darkness; the sorcerer seemed to
appear from nowhere when he stepped forward.

Hiding in the shadows to make a mysterious
entrance, Dayven thought scornfully. A wizard's trick.
He wiped his damp palms on his tunic.

The sorcerer, unlike the doorkeeper, was everything a wizard should be. Strange symbols, embroidered in silver, shimmered over his gray robe, and his
long beard floated around him. He stared at Dayven a
moment and then blinked, just as the owl had.

"Sit there, boy," he commanded, pointing to a stool

at the end of the table by the skull. His voice was deep and sonorous. "Before we begin, you must swear never to reveal what passes in this room to anyone who has not taken the test themselves."

"I do so swear." Dayven had expected that, but he was surprised the oath was so straightforward. No threats of hideous vengeance if he broke his word? No spells to compel his silence?

"Very well. The test for sorcerous ability is a simple one, at least on your part. For us it is somewhat more complex. As you watch, we will work several acts of magic—some greater, some lesser. When we have finished, you must try to tell us which act of magic was the greatest. Is that clear?"

"Perfectly." For the first time, Dayven felt a flicker of confidence. Even if he should see a great act of magic, he didn't have to tell them what it was. Lying was against the Guardian's creed, but wizards had no honor, so Dayven felt few qualms about lying to them. His oath to his mother was far more important than lying to a few wizards.

"Then we shall begin. You must remain seated. Do not interrupt us, no matter what happens. The test may be simple, but it is not without danger. Our concentration, and yours, must be complete."

Dayven nodded. He had no wish to interrupt anything. As soon as this was over he could go back to the palace and get on with his chores. He was missing jousting practice this morning, and—

"We begin," said the sorcerer abruptly. The doorkeeper lifted the brazier to the end of the table opposite Dayven. The coals' soft glow set red eyes winking in the shining bottles that lined the shelves.

"First, we prepare the air," said the sorcerer. He plucked a bundle of herbs from the ceiling and scattered them on the coals. Thick smoke filled the room; it smelled vile. Dayven suppressed a cough, but the smoke didn't seem to bother the sorcerer. Instead of dissipating like normal smoke, it lingered around them in drifts and coils.

"We begin the elixir," the sorcerer half-chanted. The doorkeeper held up a bowl and the sorcerer emptied a flask of thick, clear liquid into it.

"Now the blood," he commanded.

The doorkeeper carried the bowl around the table and set it beside Dayven, pulling a small, sharp knife from his pocket. "Give me your hand. No, not the right, the left one." He grasped Dayven's little finger and pricked it. Then he squeezed it over the bowl until three drops of Dayven's blood had fallen. They lay on top of the liquid, like oil on water.

Next the doorkeeper lifted the skull. Dayven flinched in spite of himself, but the doorkeeper only picked up a small vial of pale green fluid that had been concealed inside it.

"Pour it in," he commanded, giving the vial to Dayven. The doorkeeper held the bowl in front of him, its contents sloshing gently. As the green liquid touched the clear, its color changed to a dark red. As soon as the vial was empty, the doorkeeper took the bowl back to the sorcerer.

A crystal ball lay on the table. *The sorcerer must have put it there when I was watching the elixir change,* Dayven thought, ignoring a twinge of uneasy doubt.

"Now the air must be transformed," the sorcerer intoned. He reached for one of the potted plants and quickly snapped off half dozen big leaves. Sap wept from the wounds and the leaves crackled as the brazier consumed them.

A new stench filled the room, stinging Dayven's eyes. His cut finger throbbed.

"Now," cried the sorcerer deeply. "Now is the proper time." He stepped forward and dashed the elixir over the crystal sphere. The liquid flowed sluggishly over the

12

crystal, which glowed red in the dim light. Then, as the sorcerer and the doorkeeper stood back, the ball jiggled, lifted right out of its stand and floated, about four inches above the table.

Dayven gasped and the ruby sphere began to move, slowly at first, in an odd, swinging circle.

The tips of Dayven's fingers began to tingle. His eyes were on the crystal as it rose slightly, moving faster. The skin of his face tingled too. But some instinct told him that it wasn't the crystal that caused it.

The floating crystal faded from his consciousness as his eyes were drawn to the sorcerer's hands. The wizard held the plant he had torn, his fingers moving gently up and down the stem. Dayven, watching intently now, saw a small flare of white light as the wizard's finger rested for a moment against one of the wounds left by the torn-out leaves. When his hand moved on, the sap no longer flowed. It was healed.

Dayven looked up and met the sorcerer's eyes.

"Enough," said the old man quietly. "Open the windows. It stinks in here."

The doorkeeper threw open the shutters and a fresh breeze dispersed the smoke. The spinning ball circled to a stop. Sunlight gleamed in the red-stained crystal . . .

and revealed the black thread that supported it.

"It was a trick," whispered Dayven. "It was all a filthy wizard's trick."

"Not all," said the sorcerer. His voice was not as deep as it had been. "I worked one act of true magic in this room. And you noticed it."

Dayven opened his mouth to deny it, he *had* to deny it, but the words wouldn't come. He had seen what he had seen, and they both knew it.

"I'm not a wizard." His voice shook and he struggled to steady it. "I can't be. I *won't* be."

"You don't have to be," said the old man calmly, "if you truly don't want to. But it has been my experience that magic finds its way to you, sooner or later. What you have is a gift, boy. Not a curse."

"I'm leaving." Dayven stood abruptly. "Now." His knees quivered. He had to get out of there.

"You are free to come and go as you like," the sorcerer told him. "But first come here. No tricks," he added as Dayven eyed him warily. "But you shouldn't decide to reject sorcery without knowing what you're rejecting. Come here."

It was a command. There was a tower full of wizards between Dayven and the street. He hesitated a moment, then moved to stand before the sorcerer.

"Give me your hand. No, the left one." Like the doorkeeper, the sorcerer reached out and took Dayven's little finger. The small cut throbbed.

"It hurts, doesn't it? Still, the memory of wellness is there, in the flesh itself. Remember. Concentrate on what it felt like when the skin was whole."

Dayven tried to pull his hand away. The sorcerer held him firmly.

"I only want to heal your finger, boy. Do as I ask and you can go."

Dayven desperately wanted to leave, so he surrendered his hand to the other's clasp.

"Think of your flesh whole, the way it should be." The sorcerer's dry finger ran gently over the cut. *Once it was healed, Dayven could go. Wizards healed people all the time.* He took a deep breath and tried to concentrate.

The strange tingling began again, not in his face and fingertips now, but in the center of his being. Dayven gasped and tried to pull free; the sorcerer's grip tightened. The tingling grew, welling to a flash of white fire that ran through his arm to the tip of his little finger, lingered there, and vanished.

Dayven's eyes met the old sorcerer's and again knowledge passed between them. The power, the magic, might have been called forth and directed by the sorcerer's skill, but it had come from Dayven. His stomach contracted, as if he were standing on a cliff edge, feeling the earth crumble from beneath his feet . . . as if his destiny was changing, twisting out of its true path. He pulled his hand from the sorcerer's grip and looked at his finger.

The cut was gone.

CHAPTER TWO

D AYVEN HUDDLED ON the corner of his bed and stared at the wall, waiting for Soren. He had run through half the town in his wild flight from the sorcerer's tower, bumping into people, knocking things over. His only thought had been to seek refuge in the room he shared with his cousin, in the wing of the palace where all the Watcherlads lived. The result of his test would have spread through the city faster than fire-wind. It always did, when the wizards found someone. Soren must have heard the news by now. So where was he?

Dayven studied his finger broodingly—there was no trace of the cut. He shuddered, remembering the terror of watching his destiny contort, dragging him helplessly to a fate he didn't want. Surely wizards, like all those who failed to follow their true paths, became ghosts: only the true path led to the next world. Once your spirit lost its way, it was lost forever. At least, that was what Lore Master Senna said. Dayven shuddered again. And yet . . . the power had come from him. The memory of welling white fire possessed him and he jumped when Soren burst through the door.

"Dayven, Lord Enar wants to see you! Is your tunic clean?"

"The Lordowner wants to see *me*?" Dayven glanced at his tunic blankly. Then bitterness filled him. "Why? Is he going to congratulate me personally? Don't you want to congratulate me?"

"I'm sorry," said Soren. "When I heard about the test, I thought we might need some help."

"We." The ache of relief replaced that of loneliness. Dayven's eyes misted and he blinked hard.

"Don't be silly." Soren reached out and gripped his shoulder. "Surely you didn't think I'd desert you? Anyway, I went to the Lore Master, to ask his advice, and he took me straight to the Lordowner. And *he* wants to see you right away, so come on!"

Soren pulled Dayven to his feet and hauled him out the door. The late-afternoon sun made his cousin's hair shine like pale gold. It was something Dayven, who was all nut brown, had always envied. But now there were

18

other things on his mind. "Master Senna wants to help me?" he repeated. "Why? I know I . . . I can't be a Guardian anymore. What could Lord Enar want with me?"

"That isn't true," said Soren. "That you can't be a Guardian, I mean. The Lore Master said you aren't committed to wizardry as long as you 'have never worked a trick of magic that will alter the destiny of any man.'"

Dayven stopped, staring at his cousin in astonishment.

"Lore Master Senna said that? I thought if you had magic in you, you didn't have a choice."

Soren shook his head. "I keep telling you, the Lore Master wants to help you. He told me you still have a choice. As long as you haven't altered anyone's destiny by magic, you can still take the Guardian's oath. And in the oath you foreswear any use of magic, except to be healed by it, so after that it doesn't matter. But the Lore Master also said that to the best of his knowledge, no one has ever shown the ability and not become a wizard. And he knew stories about people who tried, Dayven. He said it was as if magic exerted a seduction that even the most dedicated couldn't resist."

The tiny thread of hope hurt almost as much as

despair, but Dayven was certain *he* could resist. If only . . .

"Is that why Lord Enar wants to see me? To give me a chance? We've been Watcherlads in his court for years, but he never noticed me before. He has dozens of Watcherlads. Why would he care that I . . . that the wizards want me?"

"I don't know," said Soren. "But he was truly interested, not just feeling sorry for you. If it didn't sound so crazy, I'd swear he was pleased." He guided Dayven around a corner and started up a small flight of stairs.

"Is your tunic clean?" Soren asked again. This time he really looked at it. Dayven was too nervous to care.

"This is the Lordowner's private chamber," he protested as they reached the landing.

"I know." Soren knocked briskly on the door. "He's waiting for us."

Lore Master Senna opened the door.

"Master Senna." Dayven bowed.

Unless he had something worth saying, the Lore Master seldom bothered with what he called "useless words." Now he simply nodded and gestured them to the chair where the Lordowner waited.

Soren hesitated and Master Senna gestured him

forward as well, so Dayven and his cousin approached the Lordowner together. Lord Enar was a big man; his strong hands and heavy shoulders made the tall rockoak staff of the herdowner that leaned against his chair look like, well, not a toy, but something he could wield with ease. As a boy, training to be a Watcherlad, Dayven had waited on him at dinner, so he was familiar with the Lordowner's booming voice. But he had never had Lord Enar's full attention focused on him, as it was now. It took an effort, as he straightened from his bow, to keep his knees from knocking.

"So you're the lad that might become a wizard," Lord Enar rumbled. "Dayven . . . son of Bran, aren't you? I remember your father. He was a good Guardian."

"That's what I want to be," said Dayven. "A good Guardian. I don't want to be a wizard, Lord."

"Hmm. Your father died in battle, as I recall. Against the Cenzar. How do you feel about that?"

Dayven started at the change of subject. "I . . . I regret that he died before I was old enough to remember him, but to fight for the Lordowner, to hold his lands and herds, is a Guardian's duty and his destiny." His father's death had been honorable, and all his father's ancestors had been respectable, too. Why had Lord Enar asked this?

Lord Enar frowned. "I meant, how do you feel about the Cenzar?"

The Cenzar? "They're the enemy, Lord. Though I understand they're brave in battle." The Cenzar had lived in this valley before the Tharn found it, just as the ancient prophecy foretold. They were driven out in Dayven's great-grandfather's time, but they'd been trying to get the valley back ever since. Soren said that if the Cenzar believed in destiny, instead of their absurd goddess, they'd have seen sense and given up by now.

Lord Enar looked at Master Senna, who was also his chief advisor, and raised his bushy eyebrows. "What do you think? I'm a soldier, not a schemer, but that sounds like honesty to me."

"He's had no reason to lie, as yet," said Master Senna dryly. "More to the point, Dayven, how do you feel about wizards?"

"I hate them!" Dayven replied instantly. "They're sly and cowardly, and have no creed. They never go into battle and fight honestly, man to man. They trick people and try to alter their destinies through magic. But I won't let them do it to me."

Lord Enar smiled at the Lore Master. "That good enough for you?"

Master Senna's eyes were fixed on Dayven's face.

"But their magic—doesn't the magic tempt you?"

The memory of white fire rose in his mind, but Dayven crushed it down. "No," he said fiercely.

"It tempted your grandmother . . ." Master Senna's voice was very soft.

"But I'm not like that!" Dayven burst out. "Wizards are craven and treacherous. I could never be like that."

The butt of the staff thudded resoundingly on the floor, drawing all eyes. "Adina's crime was treason, not wizardry," the Lordowner pronounced. "And we'll have no injustice done her descendants in my hall. She paid for her crime, and that ends it. Besides, there are wizards in other lands who have never betrayed their overlords. What matters now, Dayven, is not whether magic tempts you, but whether you can be loyal, and I think you can. I have a favor to ask you. It's more than I like to ask of a boy your age, but as far as I can see, you're the only person who might succeed. Since you've already been accepted into their herd, so to speak."

"I'm ready to obey, Lord, but I don't understand. What do you want me to do?"

"I want you to spy on the wizards for me," said Lord Enar bluntly. "I want you to study with them. Wear their gray robes. Learn their intentions and report back to me. You can write to your cousin," he nodded to

Soren, "without arousing their suspicion, and he can pass the information on. But aside from the people in this room, no one must learn the truth of this. *No one.* Or you'll be useless as a spy."

Dayven's heart sank. Spy on the wizards? "But why? They're your wizards, Lord."

Lord Enar grimaced. "As you said, wizards have no creed—they're loyal to no one but themselves. Ordinarily they take no interest in affairs of state, but I'm afraid that these wizards may be in league with the Cenzar."

Dayven stared at him, shocked. "Then why don't you kill them? Or at least throw them out?"

Lord Enar glanced triumphantly at Master Senna. "Because I might be wrong," he admitted. "We know the Cenzar are gathering troops for a great attack, perhaps the strongest army they've sent against us. The wizards themselves reported it. The Cenzar don't let wizards live in their city, though they sometimes allow them to visit because of their healing powers. But in spite of their ability to visit the Cenzar camps, they give me precious little information. I ask about troop strength, I get nothing but wizardly double-talk. So I've begun to doubt them.

"Forty years ago, they tried to overthrow my father

and put a man they could control in his place. We barely discovered their plot in time."

Dayven struggled not to wince. That was the plot for which his grandmother had died. Lord Enar knew about that, and he was still willing to trust Dayven with this? The Lordowner might be a soldier, rather than a subtle schemer, but he understood men's hearts far better then Master Senna did.

"Their power was broken then," Lord Enar continued. "But if they're plotting with the Cenzar now . . . I'd be tempted to kill them, or drive them out, but we need their healing powers. In battle, having wizards on your side can mean the difference between winning and losing. And if they are loyal, in their odd way, to punish them would be a great injustice. On the other hand, suppose the Cenzar use them against us in battle? I can't risk that."

"How could they use wizards in battle?" asked Dayven. "Wizards are cowards. They never fight."

"Suppose," said Lord Enar. "Suppose they could fight from a distance. With magic. No one has ever been sure of the true extent of their powers. At the moment I'm not even sure of their loyalty. That's why I need a man on the inside, and I think you're the one for the job."

"But they'll want me to learn magic," Dayven

protested. "I promised my . . . I once swore to have nothing to do with wizards. I want to be a Guardian."

"The first rule of the Guardian's creed," said Lord Enar, "is defending those weaker than yourself. Even when it's hard. Especially when it's hard."

"But if he learns magic . . ." Soren spoke for the first time.

"It isn't knowing magic that's wrong," said Master Senna. "It's using it to alter what was destined to be. The great evil of wizards is not their gift, but their refusal to accept the way things are, instead of the way wizards think they should be. If your desire to become a Guardian holds true, you might succeed." *Might.* His cool gaze searched Dayven's face, and Dayven stared back defiantly.

"You'll only be with them until you learn the truth," Lord Enar promised heartily. "Or until the Cenzar attack, and judging by what I've learned of the army they're raising, that will happen within the year. And you won't lose by it. If you succeed, you'll get your sword and whistle from my own hands. Fates, you'll have earned it! Well, boy? What do you say?"

Dayven had sworn to have nothing to do with wizards. But he had also sworn to serve the Lordowner. Honor is loyalty. *This was a test fit for a Guardian!*

"I'll do it."

"It may be harder than you think," Lord Enar warned him. "It's become known that you have magic in you. No Tharn will have much respect for a would-be wizard. If you want to convince the wizards you're going to join them you'll have to convince everyone in the castle first, and the town too. The wizards have ears everywhere. You'll be despised by your friends. And your enemies will gloat, which is worse. But I forbid you to brawl over this, no matter what anyone says. Understand?"

"I'm afraid not," said Dayven. "Wouldn't getting into a fight with someone give me more reason to join the wizards?"

"Maybe. But if you start defending yourself with your fists, you may start defending yourself with words, and there's too much danger the truth will slip out. No fighting."

"Yes, Lord."

Dayven sat at the long table, his hands clenched around his knife and fork, his eyes fixed on his untouched plate. The scent of well-cooked roast, usually so appetizing, meant nothing to him. He was trying to identify the origin of the almost inaudible whisper that had followed him throughout the meal. He knew that he should ignore it. Soon he'd be gone, and when he returned he'd be made a Guardian, and the whispers would end forever. But he couldn't ignore it.

The constant run of Soren's voice made it harder for him to hear. From the moment they entered the dining hall, and every Guardian and Watcherlad took one look at him and turned away, Soren had been speaking—a nonstop stream of aimless chatter that required no reply.

Soren didn't want him to find out who was doing the whispering, and Soren was probably right. He had promised Lord Enar: no fighting. But he could, with honor, figure out who it was for the future, couldn't he?

One whisper had been growing louder for the last half hour, and it was starting to overwhelm his cousin's voice. Eyes down and body rigid, Dayven sought to identify the source of the fragmented insults.

". . . she was hanged of course . . ." Dayven could almost make it out now. ". . . knew . . . bad blood in both of them . . . mother's side of . . . she was always such a proper slut."

Dayven snapped to his feet and spun around.

Soren grabbed his arm, murmuring urgently about duty and missions. Dayven didn't care.

In all the hall only one pair of eyes met his, taunting him silently. Benen. Benen, whose father was such a wastrel he'd chosen to call himself his mother's son; who had always been jealous of Soren's swordsmanship, his skill with horse and lance. And he was sly as a wizard. Just the kind to whisper behind your back the insults he wouldn't dare say to your face. If the truth were known he'd—

Jerking his arm, Soren turned Dayven toward the high table at the end of the room.

Lord Enar was looking at him. Burly and commanding, he held Dayven's gaze until Dayven's eyes dropped. Obedience to the Lordowner was the Guardian's second rule. *Very well, Lord,* Dayven promised silently. *My loyalty will prove my honor. I will pass your test. I will catch these wizards at their treachery and put a stop to them. I will be the Guardian my mother wanted me to be, and I will redeem the disgrace my grandmother brought upon us. And the cowards who are whispering now will eat their words with pepper sauce!*

The next morning he stood with Soren by the castle gate, his pack dragging at his shoulders. They had spent most of the night packing Dayven's clothes and discussing the difficulties he would face.

"I still think the hardest part will be to convince the wizards you really want to be one of them," Soren fretted. "After the way you ran out of there yesterday—"

"I'll tell them that when the others found out I could work magic, they rejected me," Dayven said. "They'll believe that. It's true."

"Don't let it bother you too much," said his cousin. "When this is finished, you'll be a hero. When you come back . . ." He paused and a shadow crossed his face.

"Soren?"

"I'm sorry, I just suddenly . . . You will come back, won't you?"

"Of course I will. I'm only moving across town."

"You think that now," said Soren. "But I've been feeling all night like you're going farther, somehow. That your destiny is changing."

A cold shiver rolled down Dayven's spine. He had often thought Soren had a touch of the seer's gift, though his cousin denied it. The seer's gift was said to be akin to wizardry, but since it revealed destiny instead of changing it, it held no dishonor. Indeed, many bards were said to have a trace of it.

"Destiny can't change," said Dayven stoutly, rejecting fear. "You follow your true path or turn from it, that's all. I'm going to follow mine. With courage and good cheer." It was the third rule.

Soren still looked worried.

"I'll come back," said Dayven. "I promise."

"But you're breaking your oath to your mother now, aren't you?"

"Do you doubt my honor?" Dayven started away.

"No, of course not." Soren caught his arm. "I understand that you had to make a choice. And your choice was right. But it shouldn't be like that, Dayven. You shouldn't have to choose between oaths. Maybe that's why I feel . . . uneasy."

"Well, don't. My loyalty is to the Lordowner and my people, oath or no oath. No wizard's trickery will ever change that, I swear it."

CHAPTER THREE

"**N**OW YOU WANT to be a wizard?" The sorcerer's embroidered robe had been replaced by one of plain gray homespun, even shabbier than the doorkeeper's. "You changed your mind in a hurry."

"I didn't have much choice," said Dayven. "Once they learned I had magic, the others wouldn't accept me. Who wants a Watcherlad that's half wizard? Who would sponsor my Guardianship?" It was disturbingly easy to sound bitter. When his training as a Watcherlad was complete, the Guardian who gave him the sword and whistle would undertake his final training—and any stain on Dayven's honor would reflect on his sponsor as well. Would any Guardian risk taking on a boy who had the ability to work magic?

"It seems to me," said the sorcerer, "that if you

endured for a time, people would eventually forget you have the gift. Especially since you wouldn't be able to use it, not knowing how. Whether *you* would be able to forget, that's another matter."

"I won't go back," said Dayven. He tried to sound sincere. "Besides, what you showed me before, it was . . . interesting."

The sorcerer rolled his eyes in exasperation. He looked at the doorkeeper. The doorkeeper shrugged.

"Very well," said the sorcerer. "There aren't many people with magical ability—we can't afford to waste one. I'll assign you a tutor. You will assist and serve him, and in return he'll teach you the proper use of your power. I think I'll assign you to Reddick."

The doorkeeper's brows rose. "But Reddick was chosen . . . I mean, is Reddick the most, umm, reliable person to put in charge of an apprentice?"

"Oh, I think so," said the sorcerer placidly. "Perhaps the responsibility will steady him. And I think he's the right one for Dayven here, which is more important.

"Your first task as an apprentice, lad, will be to find your master and tell him that I want to see him immediately."

"If you want Reddick to leave town," said the doorkeeper, "we'll have to pay for it."

"Really? How tiresome. Get the money; the boy can take it."

The doorkeeper left.

"Umm, Master, I don't understand. Is my tutor going somewhere? Do you pay him to work for you?"

"Reddick is usually traveling. He's a bit of a rover, I'm afraid."

"Why do you have to pay him?" Dayven persisted. "Isn't he loyal to you?"

"Reddick's very loyal. And the money isn't a payment. At least, not to Reddick."

"But—"

"I've got it." The doorkeeper reappeared, a jingling bag in his hands. "Come with me."

At the tower door he handed the money to Dayven. "You can leave your pack with us. Don't forget he's supposed to come *here* before he sets out. It's up to you to make sure he does."

"But where do I find him? What's this money for?"

"Bail," said the doorkeeper, grinning. "Your tutor's in the cells. As his apprentice, it's your duty to buy him out. And don't forget to bring him back here!"

"What's he in for?" asked Dayven as he followed the guard down the uneven steps. The sorcerer's money had proved sufficient to pay his tutor's fine.

"Brawling. Drunk in public. Disrespect to the authorities. The usual," said the guard. "He's a regular down here. Hey, Reddick!" He unlocked one of the doors. "Time to go."

A messy heap of cloth and straw in the corner of the cell stirred and a face emerged. The hair was the same color as the dirty straw, and the short, thick beard was tangled as a briar bush. The eyes were bloodshot.

"You pox-ridden son-of-a-snake," said Dayven's new tutor. "Can't this wait till I sleep it off?"

"No," said the guard amiably. "On your feet, sot. You're evicted. Your fine's paid. We need the space for better men."

"What day is this? Thirdday? What jackass would waste good money just to get me out two days early? Who's the kid?" Reddick stood, brushing straw from his robes. He was short and stocky; half muscle, half fat, Dayven guessed. His shoulders were broad as a bull's.

"The wizards paid your fine," Dayven told him coldly. "They want to see you immediately."

"Which wizard?" Reddick emerged from the cell, wincing at the light from the high window. "Those prune-faced old skints never passed the hat just to get me out of this rat-hole." He gave the guard a friendly clap on the back that made the man totter, and started rapidly down the corridor to the stairs. Dayven had to run to catch him.

"The wizards want to see you immediately." His voice was rising. "Now."

Reddick stopped walking. He reached out and gripped the collar of Dayven's tunic; his fist was almost as big as Dayven's face.

"Let me give you some real good advice. Never yell at a man who's sousing-sick. It makes us testy. I've spent a night and a day in this sty, and I'm hungry and dry as a desert. I'm going to a tavern. You want to come, keep your voice down. Got it?"

When he let go of Dayven's tunic, the boy staggered. Reddick plodded up the stairs, leaving Dayven staring after him.

"Close your mouth or the flies'll get in," said the guard, coming up beside him.

Dayven closed his mouth and followed Reddick up the stairs.

When he reached the street, the wizard wasn't there, but it wasn't hard to guess where the sot had gone. Dayven looked for the nearest tavern; it was three doors down and the barmaid was slapping Reddick's hand as Dayven walked in.

"None of that, you saucy scoundrel," she said cheerfully. "And no food or drink either, unless you pay something on your tab."

"You'd be that cruel to a starving man?" The rough voice was unspeakably pathetic.

"Huh! They feed you three meals a day in the cells, you make-bait, and well I know it."

"That slop," said Reddick. "I couldn't eat a bite. Not knowing that your cooking was only moments away."

"Sure." The barmaid went back to the tankards she was washing.

"True as fate," the wizard swore. "I hungered for your cooking as a bee hungers for the first flower of spring."

"You liar." The barmaid shook her dishrag at him. Reddick held up his hands in mock defense, laughing. When the girl turned back, a flower lay in one of the newly washed tankards.

She and Dayven both gasped.

Dayven stared at his fingertips. He hadn't felt any tingling. He looked more closely at the flower—he'd seen dozens like it blooming in a window box in front of the shop next to the jail. *Just another wizard's trick.* He scowled.

The barmaid smiled. "Your tab is so large already, I

guess one more meal won't make any difference."

"Two," Reddick called after her as she started for the kitchen. "One for the kid, as well."

"So you think you want to be my apprentice." Reddick finished the last of his stew and leaned back in his chair, cradling a tankard of ale in his big hands. "Since those snot-nosed Guardians gave you the cold shoulder and you decided being a wizard was the only thing left."

Dayven winced, but he couldn't think of any other way to put it that wasn't a lie. The wizard looked better now that he'd eaten. Dayven himself felt better for the meal, but he had a task to perform.

"Will you go to the Master Sorcerer now? They said to be sure you saw him before you left. Are you going somewhere?"

"I'm always going somewhere. And the old geezer's not the 'Master Sorcerer.' No titles, no rank. You're an apprentice, and then you're a wizard. That's it. His name is Sundar, if you want to use it."

"I thought he was in charge," said Dayven. "Who is your leader then?"

"No leader." Reddick pushed his chair aside and stood. "We got a council, for all the good it does." He hugged the barmaid. "I'll be back," he told her. "I couldn't stay away from the best food in the city. Someday I might even pay for it." He easily avoided her slap and strode into the street.

Dayven scrambled after him. "Where are we going?"

"To see Sundar. You said he paid my fine. I owe him."

"I think he has a quest for you," Dayven told him. "Do you go on quests for the wizards?"

"Wizards don't have quests, kid. Only Guardians go on quests. You know that."

"A mission then? An errand?"

"Oh, great." The big wizard stopped and glared at Dayven. "Do I strike you as an errand boy?"

"Actually . . . Ah . . . no, Master."

"Forget that master stuff." The big man turned and strode on. "Name's Reddick. You got something to ride?"

"I can get a horse," said Dayven.

"Then do it. Pack your stuff and food for a week and meet me in the stables at the wizard's compound. I won't take long with Sundar. We'll leave in an hour or so. You got enough money left to pay for the food?"

"Yes, but where are we going?"

"You're not going anywhere unless you get packed."

"I've already packed, but—"

"What kind of apprentice are you? I give you an order and you argue about it. If you're not ready to leave when I am, I'll leave without you."

"But—"

"Go!" Reddick strode away.

Dayven's jaw clenched as he watched Reddick move through the crowd. How dare that scruffy sot of a wizard give him orders? He was Watcherlad to the Lordowner . . . *No, he was a spy for the Lordowner.* And he'd better stop thinking like a Watcherlad and start acting like a wizard's apprentice if he wanted to succeed. At least this careless drunkard would be easy to fool. Dayven turned and started back to the castle to find himself a horse.

Reddick was waiting at the wizards' compound gate when Dayven rode up. He had Dayven's pack in one hand, and a drab brown robe in the other.

"Here, put this on," he said, tossing the robe to Dayven. "I'm not traveling with someone dressed like a Guardian's messenger."

"Why is this robe brown instead of gray?" Dayven eyed the coarse brown fabric with distaste. He had left his Watcherlad's tabard, embroidered with Lord Enar's sigil, in his room, but his britches and shirt were cooler and more practical than a robe. Besides, only wizards wore robes, no matter what their color.

"Because brown cloth is cheap. Only wizards wear gray. Most apprentices wear brown, but you can wear any color you want. You got another robe?"

"No."

"Then wear that."

Dayven began to work his way into the voluminous garment and made a discovery. "Why has it got so many pockets?" Dozens of pockets. One was large enough to hold a thick book, and another so small he could barely insert two fingers.

"To carry things in. Most wizards are pack rats. In a few weeks, you'll probably be wishing for more of them."

Dayven pulled the robe over his head. "I'd rather carry my things in my . . . What are you doing with my pack?"

"Loading it." Reddick fastened the pack to Dayven's saddle with practiced ease. "We're leaving. We can make quite a few miles before the light goes."

"Leaving now? But—"

"But what?" Reddick mounted his leggy mule and rode off toward the city gate. "You're my apprentice, right? You go where I go. How else can I teach you?"

41

Dayven spurred forward and grabbed the mule's rein just above the bit, pulling the animal to a stop.

"Where," he said distinctly, "are we going?"

"Is that what you've been fussing about? Why didn't you ask? We're going to spy on the Cenzar."

Reddick pulled his reins from Dayven's slackened grasp and rode off.

Dayven gritted his teeth and followed the wizard.

CHAPTER FOUR

"HY ARE WE GOING to spy on the Cenzar?" Though Dayven would never have admitted it, the rustling jinot trees and the waking night-birds' strange calls were a little unnerving if you were city bred. He gazed around the clearing where Reddick had chosen to camp. The wizard seemed perfectly at home.

"Look at this stuff." Reddick had gathered an armload of the jinot's wafer-thin bark. Now he held up a strip. The fading orange sunset glowed through it.

"It's jinot bark. So what?" Dayven had spent most of the day brooding over being whisked out of town without being given a chance to tell Lord Enar where he was going, though he'd given one of the grooms a note for Soren when he'd gotten his horse. That should seem natural, even if the wizards suspected him. But he

43

wouldn't be able to write to his cousin from the Cenzar city—no messengers rode between the enemy strongholds. If he had urgent news . . . He'd find a way.

"For one thing," said Reddick, "jinot bark isn't really bark. If you dig through the dry outer layers to the green ones, you can peel it in sheets. But they're still thin as gossamer. That whole huge tree is composed of this stuff." He put the bark down by the wood Dayven had gathered. Then he crumpled a handful and placed it in the fire pit between their bedrolls.

Dayven glanced at a shaggy jinot trunk; it looked like it was shedding.

"So what?" he repeated wearily. "Why don't you ever answer my questions?"

"Jinot bark is also good for starting fires." Reddick pulled flint and steel from his pack and began to strike sparks into the feathery bark. "Why don't I answer your question about the Cenzar?" A spark caught and smoldered—Reddick dropped the flint and steel and blew on it gently.

"The answer should be obvious," he continued between breaths. "We're spying on them because they're gathering an army to attack us."

Attack *us*. Did that mean the wizard truly considered the Cenzar an enemy? Or was he lying to fool

44

Dayven? Or just offering another obvious, meaningless answer to drive his apprentice insane? If so, it was working.

Smoke rose from the jinot and embers glowed. Reddick blew again, carefully, and the bark burst into flame. Reddick began to pile small sticks on it. "That's a lot harder to do with regular wood," he said with satisfaction.

"I meant," said Dayven with all the patience he could muster, "why are *we* going to spy on the Cenzar?"

"Ah. Why didn't you say so?"

Dayven gritted his teeth and the wizard grinned.

"I'm going because I've traveled with the Cenzar. I have friends in the city who'll vouch for me." Reddick added bigger sticks to the fire. "You're going because, first, you're my apprentice and I can't teach you if we're not together, and second, I think I can get you into a *zondar*."

Dayven blinked at the unfamiliar word and Reddick's brows lifted. "You do speak Cenzar, don't you?"

"Of course," said Dayven. "You have to, to talk to the peasants. But I don't know that word. What's a zondar?"

"A school for warriors. They'll be about your own

45

age. You can study with them—learn how a Cenzar fighter is trained."

Dayven frowned. "Why do we need to know that? They're brave, for barbarians, but we've beaten them before."

Reddick sighed. "It's not that simple. We've always beaten them before because we had them outnumbered, but fighting isn't just a matter of bravery, it's a matter of method. Didn't your Sword Master teach you to observe your opponent's weaknesses so you can use them against him?"

Dayven nodded.

"Well, we haven't fought the Cenzar since you were a baby. You can help us find out their weaknesses. Get into your blankets now. It's getting chilly, and we're starting early tomorrow."

Dayven wiggled into his bedroll. The long wizard's robe twisted around him and he wiggled some more to untangle it. Reddick chuckled.

"What will you be doing while I'm in school?" asked Dayven. "Is it really so important to learn how the Cenzar train?"

"Of course it is," said Reddick. "The more you know about anything . . . Here, let me show you." He pulled a handful of jinot bark from the woodpile.

Dayven felt the faint tingling in the skin of his face, but he still gasped when the bark burst into flame.

Reddick cupped the burning bark in his hands. His expression, as he stared into the fire, was thoughtful and content. The bark burned for several minutes before it flickered out. Reddick brushed the ashes from his hands and held them out to Dayven, slightly smudged, but with no trace of a burn to show where the fire had been.

"If you understand something, really understand it, it will hardly ever hurt you," he said peacefully.

"But—"

"No more questions tonight." Reddick rolled into his own blankets. "Get some sleep."

"But why did you use flint and steel instead of lighting the fire with magic?"

"Magic takes more energy." Reddick yawned.

"Are you going to teach me magic?" Dayven asked. His stomach twisted at the thought. *A would-be Guardian shouldn't do this. Though Lord Enar had said—*

"Sure," said Reddick. "Tomorrow. Don't forget to keep the fire going."

In just a few minutes the wizard's snores filled the small camp.

Dayven lay awake. *Lord Enar had said it was all right*

to learn magic as long as he was loyal—and there was no doubt of that! Still . . . He wiggled silently out of his blankets, reached into the woodpile and pulled out a fistful of jinot bark. Lighting a corner, he cradled it in his hands, watching the flame grow. It scorched his palm. He dropped the blazing bark and licked the burn. Reddick continued to snore; Dayven glared at him. Then he added more wood to the fire and went to bed.

"Wake up, kid." Someone shook Dayven's shoulder. "It's time for your magic lesson."

"Huh?" Dayven dragged his eyes open. The fire crackled cheerfully, but the pot over it hadn't even begun to steam. Though the sky was lighter in the east, sunrise was at least an hour off. Dayven moaned and buried his head in his blankets.

"Come on." Reddick shook him harder. "We're going to start riding at first light. If you want a magic lesson, you've got to start now."

"Forget it," Dayven mumbled.

A firm yank stripped the covers from his body. Dayven yelped as the cold reached him. He sat up, glaring at the wizard.

"I thought Watcherlads had to be up and working

48

before dawn." Reddick grinned at him, blankets dangling from his fist. "How did you manage it?"

"Soren got me up." Dayven yawned and rubbed his face.

"Soren must have been pretty determined," said his tutor. "But you haven't seen determined till you've seen me in action. Sit up straight—I'm going to teach you to meditate."

The lesson did not go well.

"You're thinking about something," said Reddick for the third time.

Dayven opened his eyes and glared at him. "I'm doing the best I can," he said. "How can you think about nothing? If you're awake, which I'd rather not be, there's always something going on in your head. You can't just keep your mind blank—it isn't natural."

"It's not a matter of blanking your mind," Reddick explained patiently. "It's more . . . emptying yourself of thought. Not even of thought, but of fussing. You slip away from the thoughts that fret and distract you. Then you can sink into yourself until you find the power."

"Sink into myself? I live in myself already!"

"Hmm," said Reddick. "Maybe you need a focus.

Wait here a minute." He walked away from the camp.

As he listened to the wizard thrashing around in the grass and bushes, Dayven wrapped his arms around his knees and wondered what Soren was doing now. And what was *he* doing, traveling to an enemy city with a wizard who was trying to empty his mind? His destiny was Guardianship. Surely this wasn't his true path—but he had no choice. If he deliberately failed to learn, sooner or later even Reddick would become suspicious. Sundar had proved he had the gift. *Magic. His grandmother had forgotten all honor and loyalty.* Dayven shivered.

"Here." A blanket dropped over his shoulders. "It's hard to meditate when you're freezing."

Dayven jumped. "I didn't hear you come back."

"You were thinking about being scared." Reddick shrugged. "Natural enough."

Dayven glared at him. "Were you reading my mind?"

Reddick's laugh boomed out. "It was written all over your face. Forget about it. Now take this." He held out his hand.

"What is it?" Dayven reached out and lifted the papery crescent from the wizard's palm. "A cocoon? What's this for?"

50

"It's for worms," said Reddick. "They spin them and then live inside while they turn into butterflies." Dayven scowled, and Reddick chuckled and went to stir the pot. "It's going to be your focus," the wizard continued. "For your meditation. Whenever you have a few minutes, I want you to study that cocoon. Hold it. Look at it. Try to learn everything about it. Don't think of anything else. Explore it with all your mind."

Dayven stared at the small brown scrap. "It'll break as soon as I put it in my pack," he complained.

"I'll give you an empty salve pot to keep it in. And not in your pack—this is what your pockets are for. I want you to touch the coccoon a lot."

Dayven grimaced.

"Hey, kid." Reddick's voice was soft, but there was a note in it that made Dayven's eyes snap to his face. "You want to learn magic? Or do you want to turn around and go back to town?"

Back to town . . . home. Which would break his oath to the Lordowner, and destroy his only chance for Guardianship.

"Magic, sir," said Dayven hastily.

"Then do what I tell you. Come eat breakfast. We'll leave as soon as we finish."

They reached the first village in the early afternoon. The thatch-roofed houses looked like all the other peasant houses Dayven had seen. The Lady's altar was covered with sheaves of grain and near-ripe fruit, now old and withered. The offerings were the Cenzar way of showing their goddess the quality of "her" crop. The altar still looked odd to Dayven, who had spent his life in the Town-within-the-Walls. When the Tharn first conquered this valley, they'd had enough trouble subduing the Cenzar peasants to the point that they would plant, harvest, and pay the Lordowner's share. According to Master Senna, they had threatened to fight to the death if the Tharn tried to take their goddess away as well. Now the villages were peaceful and full of people—but here, the hoofbeats of their mounts, echoing off the stone walls, was the only sound.

"I don't understand." Reddick gazed at the deserted street. "All the men might be in the fields, but it's not harvest time yet. The women should be here. And where are the children?"

Dayven considered the silent houses. "Maybe they're hiding. Maybe they went somewhere."

"Just before harvest time? Where? And why? You wait here. I'm going to look around."

"I'll come with you." Dayven dismounted.

"No, I don't want to disturb anything. Meditate." The wizard flashed him a smile and was gone.

Dayven sat down, leaning against the side of a quiet house. He pulled the cocoon from his pocket; if Reddick snuck up on him again, he wanted to look as if he were doing what he was supposed to. Then Reddick would have less reason to suspect him. He gazed at the rough, drab surface of the cocoon; it was feather light. How could such a trivial thing teach him magic?

Eventually, the silence seeped into his spirit and Dayven leaned back against the wall and relaxed. He wondered what Soren was doing now. What *he'd* be doing, if he were home where he should be. His mind drifted to the white fire the sorcerer, Sundar, had called forth in him. This cocoon couldn't rouse his magic, he was sure of that. Could he admit to himself that the welling of power had been beautiful? He let the memory flood his mind. He imagined that power called forth by the cocoon, touching it—seeing it not with his hands, but with that part of his mind that sensed the flowing fire of magic. He couldn't help but want it. Impulsively, he willed it.

Suddenly his mind was inside the cocoon. He felt the papery surface against his palm, but he felt the shimmering whisper of life with his mind.

Dayven's eyes flew open. His heart hammered. He stared at the cocoon in horror.

"So it worked."

Dayven jumped and gazed up at his tutor.

"I thought it might," Reddick added. "Live things are a great focus."

"I . . . I felt . . ." Dayven's mouth was dry. "I did magic."

"You did great. Keep practicing. But now, come with me. I think I found the problem."

Reddick led him briskly down the hill to the dry streambed at the bottom. "You see? This would be enough to empty any village."

"See what?" Dayven, his mind still on the power he had called forth, looked around them. "I don't see anything."

"You're standing in it," said the wizard. "Or rather, you're not standing in it. That's the problem. The stream is dry."

"Couldn't something natural have caused it?" A branch whipped back and lashed his face; Dayven brushed it aside irritably. It was past dark now and the track beside the dry streambed was rough.

"It doesn't matter if it's natural or not," said Reddick. "Four villages depend on that stream for water, not only for themselves, but for their crops and livestock. In the village we're about to reach, it turns a mill wheel. For those villages, losing that stream is a catastrophe."

"That's their Guardian's problem, isn't it? He's the one who holds these lands for the Lordowner. Isn't it more important to learn the Cenzars' plans before they attack us?" Dayven glared at his tutor's broad back as the mule scrambled nimbly up the trail in front of him.

"It's not that simple," said Reddick, exasperated. "There's no natural reason for that stream to be dry. We haven't had a drought. Another reason is that—"

A dark form slid from the shadows and grasped Dayven's reins. A hand came from behind him and seized his wrist; more hands caught his arm before he could reach for his knife.

"What the—help!" Dayven shouted. Torches sprang to life revealing swarthy Cenzar faces—peasants. Not warriors, only peasants. The thought should have reassured Dayven, but his racing heart didn't slow . . . perhaps because the expressions on their faces were far from reassuring. Two of them held Reddick's arms behind his back while a third lashed his wrists together.

Dayven felt the harshness of rope on his own wrists.

"Take it easy," said Reddick in Cenzar. "Nobody has to get hurt here."

"I hope not," said one of the peasants gently, "for your sake, wizard."

CHAPTER FIVE

"BUT WHY DO YOU think it was magic that stopped the stream?" Reddick argued. "I agree it's not a natural cause, but that doesn't mean wizards had anything to do with it. Why would we?"

The village chieftain was an old peasant, who had welcomed them with exquisite courtesy and the steepled fingers which were the Cenzar gesture of greeting. "The stream has been faithful for centuries," he said. "In the worst of droughts it never failed entirely. Something stopped it. And wizards are meddlers."

"We're also healers," said Reddick. "We care about the land."

"For all your care the land continues to weaken," the old man retorted. "Each harvest is less than the one before."

"You know why that's happening," said Reddick. "It has nothing to do with the wizards."

"No." The chieftain's face twisted suddenly. "That is the fault of the Tharn. In their greed they force us to dishonor the Lady's ways, straining the land, destroy—"

A rumble of anger from the crowd drowned his voice and Dayven shivered. The population of four villages hemmed them in. Dayven had always considered the peasants docile people, who would never challenge their Tharn overlords, but the faces that glared in the ruddy torchlight were hard, angry, and desperate. Dayven felt a reluctant sympathy. And despite the formal offering of corncake and wine—a Cenzar custom that proclaimed them guests instead of prisoners—he felt the beginning of a fear that should have been beneath a future Guardian.

"How long ago did the stream fail?" Reddick asked. "Did it get smaller over a long period?"

"No."

"All at once."

"We just woke up and it was almost dry." Several voices spoke, almost together.

"That was nine days ago," the old man added. "It went from full to barely a trickle in the space of a night. Do you wonder that we suspect magic?"

58

"What have you done about it? Hasn't anyone gone to investigate?" Reddick asked.

"Of course. Two men from Banadeen, the village farthest upstream, set out that very morning. When three days passed and they had not returned, we agreed that all four villages would each send two more men. Six days have passed since they left. The stream is still dry and the men we sent are all missing. The crops are close to ripening; we could begin the harvest now. Indeed, we must if the steam remains dry. It will be a lean harvest. We will survive, but every hand will be needed to get the crops in before they wither. We are missing ten men. And without the mill to crush the grapes and grind the wheat and corn . . ." The chieftain shrugged.

"Why don't you ask your Guardian for help?" Dayven spoke up for the first time. "It's his duty to find out what happened to the stream and your men."

"The Tharn Guardian?" The old peasant sneered. "What does he care about the land his father conquered, except to drain it to support his herds? Tharn steel makes strong plowshares; that is the only good we get from the Tharn. . . . But we tried. When our men failed to return, we humbled ourselves and went to the Guardian. He told us he was too busy preparing for war to be bothered with 'peasant problems.' We wasted pre-cious time on him."

"Then you'd better not waste any more," said Reddick. "Start your harvest tomorrow."

"And abandon ten men to whatever fate they met?" The old man rubbed his face wearily. "I suppose we must. If we are to salvage anything from this crop we can lose no more time and spare no more hands."

A murmur of protest ran through the crowd. A woman sobbed.

"No." Reddick shook his head. "My apprentice and I will go upstream and find out what's happening. I can't promise to solve anything, but we'll do our best. At least we'll find out what's going on up there."

Dayven sat in the dry streambed, meditating on the cocoon. Reddick was preparing breakfast so he had plenty of time. In fact, after his first taste of Dayven's cooking, Reddick had taken over all the food prepara-tion. He said it would give Dayven more time to prac-tice magic. During the two days they had been traveling toward the mountain lake that was the source of the stream, Reddick made sure Dayven got lots of practice. He couldn't refuse without making the wizard suspi-cious. Now he could stretch out his mind at will and touch the life within the lifeless wrapping. He thought that if his skill was greater he could know every part of the transformation taking place in the small clay pot in his pocket. What frightened him was that he wanted to.

Dayven ran his fingers through the sand of the streambed, finding water-smoothed stones. He had told himself that learning magic wouldn't change him. But now . . .

Perhaps it was because he had lived all his life in a city that he had never realized how alive plants were, but lately he had begun to notice *stones*. Rough and smooth, and of more types than he had ever dreamed existed. Reddick had found him staring at a vein of quartz embedded in a granite hillside and explained about different rocks and how they were formed. Before, Dayven had just assumed that rock was rock. Now he was beginning to find uniqueness in them— and life in everything around him. *Had grandmother Adina seen the world like this?*

Dayven wondered what Soren would think of it, if he ever had the courage to tell him. Thinking of his cousin made Dayven long for his company and with the longing came the vision. His eyes were open, but he no longer saw the streambed and bushes. His mind filled with a picture of Soren. His cousin was standing with a

61

group of Watcherlads observing a bout in the practice yard. Judging by his sweat-stained clothes Soren had fought previously himself. Dayven couldn't see the fighters, but he could follow the progress of the combat by the changes of expression on his cousin's face. Then the struggle surged toward Soren, the ring of Watcherlads broke, and Soren leapt back, laughing. The vision vanished.

Dayven sat in the streambed; his heart pounded. He had heard of wizards spying on people from afar. Scrying, it was called. It was one of the magics people hated wizards for. Even wizards, he had heard, had rules about its use. Should he tell Reddick what happened? Master Senna had said that magic itself was not wrong, only using it to alter destiny. But he hadn't been speaking about scrying. On the other hand, scrying could be very useful to a spy. And to refuse to learn any kind of wizardry would be suspicious. For a careless sot, Reddick saw a great deal. What if there were other wizard's skills that could be turned against them? If Dayven could use magic to serve the Lordowner, then learning it was justified, wasn't it? He would no longer resist his lessons. And he wouldn't tell Reddick that he had discovered how to scry. Dayven packed the cocoon carefully in its pot and returned to camp.

✧ ✧ ✧

"We'll reach the lake soon," said Reddick. They were climbing out of a ravine the stream had cut. It was hard going for the horse; Reddick's mule was more sure-footed.

Reddick glanced at the sun. "We'll have several hours to poke around before dark, and we may need it. When I first volunteered for this, I'd hoped we wouldn't have to go all the way up."

"It'll take days to go down, too," Dayven grumbled. "It'll delay our report on the Cenzar by almost a week."

"I thought a Guardian's first duty was defending the weak," said Reddick. "What are you complaining about?"

"But you're not a Guardian," said Dayven shrewdly. "Why are we doing this?"

Reddick nodded approvingly. "You're learning, kid. We're here because the Cenzar are right when they call wizards meddlers. We're not particularly noble, but we're the worst busybodies in the world. I want to find out what happened to the stream, not to mention those men."

Dayven frowned as they emerged from the ravine. "It is a Guardian's duty to protect the weak, but sometimes other duties take precedence. Isn't information about the Cenzar's plans more important than . . . Fates!"

"What are you gaping at?" Reddick followed his gaze. A huge arc of stone ran from the top of the hill in front of them down to the ravine. It was supported by sweeping arches. In the clear light, it looked as fragile as a sculpture in glass.

"What is it?" Dayven whispered.

"A water trough," said Reddick. "Or maybe 'water bridge' is a better description. The Cenzar built it centuries ago to carry part of the river to that streambed, so they could farm the land in this part of the foothills."

Dayven blinked. "You mean there wasn't a stream there before?"

"That's right. The Cenzar came all the way up here and found the lake. But the river that drains it went down the wrong side of the mountain. So they built that," he gestured at the incredible structure, "to carry part of the river over this slope and down to the valley. Then they dug a trench and diverted part of the river. Remarkable, isn't it?"

"But the Cenzar are barbarians! How could they build something to . . . to carry a river through the air?"

"It's not carrying a river now," said Reddick. "Come on. The lake's just over that ridge."

✧ ✧ ✧

The stream had stopped because it had been dammed.

"It took us the best part of a day and a night to block it off," the Tharn captain told them. "We're fighting men, not ditch-diggers. But Lord Enar figured that if the river flooded, the Cenzar troops might have trouble crossing it. At least they'd be likely to lose some supplies. So he sent us to see if we could find a way to make the river larger. Empty the lake faster somehow, he said. I thought it was cow flop. But when we got up here it was simple. We just blocked off this trench." He gestured to the smooth-stoned canal that led from the river to the water bridge.

Dayven and Reddick had found the dam—and the two Tharn guardsmen who'd been posted there— shortly before dusk. One of them had stayed to keep an eye on the wizard and his apprentice, while his comrade went to fetch their captain.

Now Reddick gazed at the river, surging down the mountain's other side. "Captain, permit me an ignorant question or two. Like all wizards, I'm a curious man. I'm very impressed with what you've done here, but won't low-lying fields be flooded downstream?"

The answer was so obvious that Dayven stared at his tutor in astonishment.

"Of course," said the captain proudly. "A couple of swamps ought to slow those Cenzar snakes down a little."

"Wonderful," said Reddick pleasantly. "I like a man who does his duty. Do you know whether the crops are in? We passed a few villages where they seemed concerned."

"They sent some men," said the captain. "We turned them into a work crew. Why should we carry all the rocks? They put up quite a fight about our having blocked the stream, but we knocked that out of them soon enough. They're at the other side of the lake now, digging to widen the place where the lake runs into the river so we can get even more water flowing."

"Did you get permission," Dayven asked, "from the Guardians whose lands and men you're tampering with? They're responsible to the Lordowner for those crops. You can't interfere with a Guardian's duty."

"No wizard tells me what I can and can't do," said the captain. "By the Lordowner's order, the army's needs take precedence, and those farmers are working for the army now. We'll take them with us when we leave. When the Cenzar warriors come, we'll give their peasant kinfolk pikes and make the warriors waste some energy chopping them up. A chance to die in battle is more than they deserve, meddling with the destiny of the river like that."

"That's ridiculous," said Dayven. "They aren't even the ones who built the water bridge—it was their ancestors. And who's to say it wasn't the river's destiny to be divided? You were just too lazy to do your own digging, so you—"

"Poxy wizard." The guard's fist was very fast and Dayven ducked too slowly. Light exploded behind his eyes and faded into darkness.

CHAPTER SIX

"IF YOU'RE GOING TO be a wizard you've got to practice a little humility." Reddick's voice was lower than usual, but it still hurt Dayven's head. "That, or learn when to duck."

Dayven opened his eyes. The world spun. He shut them again and swallowed. "What happened?"

"I talked fast and got us out of there. We might have ended up part of the work crew, except the captain doesn't want a pair of wizards around all the time."

"He couldn't do that," said Dayven groggily. "As Lord Enar's Watcherlad, I outrank him."

"Not anymore . . . apprentice."

Dayven winced. "So now what? I suppose you'll want to warn the Guardians whose lands are threatened?"

"Not exactly," said Reddick. "The first thing we're

going to do is teach you how to heal yourself and get rid of that headache."

Dayven pressed his hand against his aching skull. "Can you heal me?"

"I could, but you're the one who will."

Dayven moaned. "I can't even think, much less work magic."

"When you feel like it least is when you need a healing spell the most. Come on, kid. Call up some power. No one's going to do it if you don't."

Dayven glared at him. "My *name* is Dayven."

"Whatever you say, kid."

"Poxy wizard," Dayven muttered. But he had decided he had no choice about learning magic.

Reddick laughed. "Come on. The memory of wholeness is still there, in the nerves, the tissue. Your body knows how to be well. It wants to be. Give it power and let it find its way."

Reddick's voice faded as Dayven turned his mind inward and sought power. It was harder, far harder, with his head aching so, but finally he found and freed it. Like slipping the cover off a jar filled with light. The light welled out and touched the pain-filled knot on the side of his head.

The throbbing nerves, the muscles, the skin—the

knowledge of how they should be was written into them, like a clerk's ledger. As the power touched them, they found their way back to wholeness. Then the light receded. Dayven opened his eyes. The pain was gone.

"Neat, huh?" said Reddick.

"It was easy," said Dayven, astonished. "Is healing always that simple?"

"Just about," Reddick told him. "Of course, that's only with injuries. And only when they're fresh. Once a wound begins to heal naturally, the flesh close to it dies; then there's nothing you can do. If the memory of the right way to be is no longer in the body, all the magic in the world can't heal it. People who aren't wizards don't understand that. They come to us with day-old wounds, sometimes with completely healed scars, and demand that we make them whole. That's what your Master Senna did. He stuck with what he thought was his true destiny until his wound became infected— he was delirious when his friends brought him to us. We saved his life, but it was too late to heal his leg."

"But the Guardian's oath allows healing," Dayven said. "I wonder why he waited."

"Maybe he wasn't as hypocritical as most," said Reddick. "Almost everyone comes to us for healing, whatever they believe. And if we can't heal them, the ones who went against their principles get even more angry. And there are other things we can't heal directly, like fevers and diseases. With a fever it's almost as if something living is trying to change the body to its own rightness. Herbs work better than magic on things like that, though magic can enhance the medicine's effect."

"Will you teach me herbs?" Dayven yawned widely.

"Healing takes a lot out of you," Reddick observed. "Get some sleep. Yes, I'll teach you about herbs, though they're harder to learn than magic. It takes years of study to understand all . . ."

Reddick's voice seemed to blur and then vanish, as Dayven faded into sleep.

The wind was blowing when he woke. The sun was just rising over the mountains that surrounded the lake. Reddick stood, staring over the water. "Feel that wind? It's blowing right out of the valley behind us and across the lake toward the river. It began just as the sun rose. A dawn wind. I bet it blows like that almost every morning. I couldn't have a more perfect setup."

"Huh? What?"

"You do wake up slow, don't you? I've got an idea,

71

how we're going to free those farmers."

"What? But what about spying on the Cenzar? If we tell the Guardians . . ."

"They probably won't do a thing. They're too busy for 'peasant problems,' remember?"

"Surely it's more important . . ." His voice trailed off before Reddick's steady gaze.

"Kid, in good conscience, as a Guardian, could you leave those men prisoners?"

Dayven's eyes fell. "No."

"Good. Then your head is worse."

"But it isn't," Dayven protested. "I feel fine."

"Oh, no you don't. In fact, you feel so bad we aren't going to be able to travel for several days. I think I'll go and tell the captain that. Get breakfast started. I shouldn't be long."

It was almost an hour before Reddick came back. Dayven put the kettle on and explored their camp. It nestled in a small clearing at the opposite side of the lake from the river, on higher ground. Once he was out of the trees Dayven could see over the water to the Tharn encampment.

He watched Reddick speaking to the captain for a long time, waving his hands persuasively. Reddick had seemed different when he was talking to the captain earlier. Meek. Almost foolish. An easy man to underestimate. The captain turned away, and the wizard bowed and went over to the peasants who were sitting with their ankles bound, eating breakfast.

Reddick spoke with each man for several minutes, then rose and left the Tharn camp. He hadn't spent long there, though it had to be important—he'd let Dayven cook.

With a sudden start, Dayven remembered he was supposed to have breakfast ready when the wizard returned. He hurried back to the clearing and poured dried oats into the bubbling kettle. The porridge wasn't quite done when Reddick arrived, but he was too satisfied to notice.

"It's going to work," he announced as he carried a small log into the camp and dropped it. It let out a loud *thock* when it fell, and Dayven realized it was hollow.

"I feel it in my bones. And it's one of the craziest schemes I ever came up with."

"What scheme?" asked Dayven. "What's that log for?"

"I'll tell you. No, better, I won't tell you. That way if . . . It'll work better if you don't know anything."

"About what?" Dayven threw the spoon into the

kettle and glared at the wizard.

"About the diversion I'm going to create tomorrow morning, while you sneak in and cut those farmers loose."

"What!"

"I just told you; tomorrow, I'm going to cause a diversion and you're going to sneak into the Tharn camp and free the farmers."

Dayven's mouth opened, but no words came out. His tutor chuckled.

"Sorry. Hey, to make it up to you, I'll teach you a new spell. How about it?"

"I am not here," Dayven muttered obediently. "I am a shadow, the wind through the grass. I am not here."

Reddick stopped carving holes in the hollow log. "I don't think you've got the idea. You're saying you're not here, but you're still projecting your presence. This doesn't make you invisible, you know. It's just a way to make people . . . overlook you. Like you were a piece of furniture or a stump. Something that ought to be there, so it isn't noticed. To do that you have to . . . contain yourself. Imagine that you're shining all over with a bright light. Then throw a cloak of power over the light so none shines out."

Dayven sighed. "It had better be a good diversion."

"It should be." Reddick's eyes sparkled. "What do you think this is?" He held up the log. It now had several holes in it.

"It looks like a flute," said Dayven. "Only it's too big for anyone to play."

"Exactly," said his tutor. "Wind pipes, they call 'em. Spookiest noise you ever heard."

"You're going to distract them by playing the flute?"

"Your hiding spell should help," Reddick told him. "If you ever master it. You can practice it up in the valley this afternoon. I want you to find me a big jinot tree. A fallen one would be good, but if you can't find one that came down recently, we'll have to whack up a live one. I'm sorry for that, but there it is."

"What do you want a jinot tree for?"

"You'll see, kid. You'll see."

Dayven lay in the bushes outside the Tharn encampment, knife in hand, trying not to shake so hard that he made the leaves rattle. His brown robe blended with the shadows in the colorless predawn light. The diversion was supposed to start at sunrise. It was almost sunrise now.

The Tharn camp was beginning to stir. The cook had

come out a few minutes ago and was building a fire. The peasants lay still, bound hand and foot in the center of the encampment, but something about their total lack of movement told Dayven they were awake and waiting. Reddick must have given them instructions when he talked to them yesterday. Dayven wished Reddick had given *him* more instructions. He wished the Guardian who warded these villages had looked after his people as he should. He wished the captain hadn't been so cruel. Dayven wouldn't have believed a Tharn officer would do something like this to people who should have been under his protection. He wished, passionately, that he was home.

Mist rose off the lake, floating wisps that spun and vanished. Dayven felt the dawn wind against his face and heard, ever so faintly, a wailing moan.

The Tharn cook heard it too. He rose and stood, looking over the lake. The mist was thickening. *Had there been mist on the water yesterday?* Dayven didn't remember it.

The wind gusted and the wind pipe sounded again, louder. Several men emerged from their tents and joined the cook; the captain was one of them.

The mist swirled in the mounting breeze. Shouldn't

the wind be blowing it off? Most of the troop had gathered, staring across the lake. Was this the diversion? No one seemed to be watching the peasants. Now? Dayven took a shaky breath and stood, slowly. No one saw him. *Now!*

"I am not here," he murmured, starting across the open ground to the bound peasants. "I am part of this place. No one has reason to notice me." He didn't believe it himself, and he was far too frightened to summon power. Giving up on magic, Dayven ran softly to the small crowd of peasants and dropped down among them. The Tharn were staring over the lake, and none of them saw him.

"This can't work," murmured a farmer. He steepled his fingers with automatic Cenzar courtesy as Dayven knelt beside him and cut frantically at the rope that bound his ankles. "I know that the Tharn believe in this foolish superstition—we spent most of yesterday making up ghost stories for them—but this is madness!"

Ghost stories? Dayven wondered. But the Tharn were talking about ghosts.

". . . makes me nervous, Captain," one of the men was saying. "I don't fear the living, you know that. But when the lost ones walk they make trouble; you know that, too."

The rope severed. The farmer rolled to his hands and knees and crept toward the bushes. His clothes were dirty enough to blend in. Dayven crawled on to the next man.

"But it's daylight!" A rising wail from across the water interrupted the captain, but he took a deep breath and continued, "I don't know what's causing the mist, or that howling, but I do know that ghosts don't walk in the day!"

"But these are Cenzar ghosts," several voices chimed in.

"Big battle fought here, exactly today."

"Ended right at dawn, it did."

"Cenzar ghosts won't like us tampering with their river."

"Peasants told us all about it."

"Look," said the captain. "We are not going to let those grimy-handed weed-pullers . . ." He gestured at the peasants.

The rising sun flashed on the blade of Dayven's knife.

He tried to run, but they caught him and dragged him back to the shore where the captain waited.

"Well, wizard brat." The wind ruffled the captain's hair and whipped the waves. He had to raise his voice to be heard over the wailing. "I suppose your master is responsible for this . . . this wizard's trickery."

Dayven set his teeth. But there was nothing to be gained by keeping silent. The plan was finished. He might as well tell the truth.

"He probably is," said Dayven. "Though I don't know what caused the mist." He gestured toward the billowing clouds. They were very thick now, and within them . . .

Dayven's voice died and he strained to see. He felt the blood drain from his face. The hard grip on his arms slackened and fell away, but he didn't move.

"Fates," Dayven whispered. "Oh my fate, not this. He summoned ghosts!"

There were forms in the mist. Transparently thin, with a greenish tinge to them, they danced and whirled, appearing and disappearing as they sailed across the lake.

Dayven's knees gave and he sank to the sand, ignoring the wild confusion around him.

The Tharn ran, some for their horses, some simply away, into the woods and down the ravine or the riverbank.

Dayven knew that the dead who had turned from destiny's true path, traitors, those who fled their enemies in battle, and even those like the Cenzar, who worshipped false gods, would become ghosts, but he had prayed never to see one. Doomed to the frustration of their nebulous half-lives, their jealousy of the living manifested itself in cruel pranks. If a ghost attached itself to a particular person, it could torment them to madness, even suicide. And these were not Tharn ghosts, but proud Cenzar warriors; Dayven could see their hawk faces and gaping death wounds. One of them floated out of the mist and drifted toward him.

Dayven closed his eyes.

A thin sheet of something damp and sticky fell over his face. He opened his eyes and pulled it off. It tore, rippling limply in the stiff breeze. The smell was familiar.

Dayven clenched his fists as rage filled him. The man-shaped forms whirled out of the mist all around him, but now he could see the clumsy cutouts for what they were.

The ghosts were layers of jinot bark!

"I just cut a man-shape out of the tree," Reddick told him. "And pulled the layers as fast as I could and tossed them into the wind."

Dayven didn't comment. He wasn't speaking to the wizard.

They were riding down a valley on the other side of the mountains, a shortcut to the Cenzar city that would make up for the time they had lost. Reddick hadn't told him about that, either, until they reached the path.

"I would have told you, but I figured you'd get caught and I knew if you didn't believe in the ghosts, they'd figure it was some kind of wizard's trick."

"Which it was," Dayven retorted. He remembered that he wasn't speaking to Reddick, but it was too late now, so he went on. "A sly, stinking, cowardly trick, with no magic in it!" Not to mention Reddick's insulting conviction that he was certain to get caught. Dayven had no intention of discussing that, ever.

"True, kid, absolutely true. I'm sorry I scared you. Really."

Dayven wasn't sure if he believed that or not. "I wish we could do more for them. Get their stream going, I mean."

"The men we freed will report to their Guardian. Maybe he'll complain to Lord Enar. Even if he doesn't, they've got a large enough crop to get by on."

"I know, but that's not how it should be. It doesn't feel right to leave like this."

Reddick laughed. "Resign yourself. Only a foo— only a Guardian would take on an army with two men, wizards or no."

Dayven gritted his teeth. Just putting up with his tutor's so-called sense of humor was a test and a half! Then something occurred to him. "Reddick, where did that mist come from?"

"From the lake. What did you think?"

"Then why didn't the wind blow it away?"

Reddick grinned and kicked his mule forward, returning no answer.

CHAPTER SEVEN

THE CITY OF THE Cenzar perched on a cliff, high above the valley floor. Dayven gasped when he first saw the sweeping walls and towers.

"It looks like the Town-within-the-Walls," he said.

"It should," Reddick told him. "Pull off here."

"Why are we stopping?" Dayven studied the fortifications. "How do you plan to get in? Sneak through the gates in disguise? Do we have disguises?"

"I knew I forgot to pack something." Reddick guided the mule behind a clump of bushes and dismounted. "Don't worry, the city admits wizards. Most places do."

"Why don't wizards live here then?" Dayven asked. Why didn't the Cenzar have their own wizards? He knew that other peoples did. "Is it something to do with their goddess?"

"Not at all," said Reddick. "Or at least, not exactly. A long time ago, the church's handmaidens used to act as judges. They said that justice came from their goddess, and her miracles proved people's guilt or innocence. But if a miracle refused to show up when the handmaidens needed one, guess what they did?"

It wasn't hard to figure out. "They faked it?"

Reddick nodded. "And it was the wizards, the old Cenzar wizards, who exposed them. The High Chieftain of that time transferred the administration of justice to his own courts, but the handmaidens still had a lot of power. They accused the wizards—accurately enough—of meddling in church matters, and that old High Chieftain may have been worried that they'd start meddling in his affairs as well. He kicked out all the Cenzar wizards. There are still a few of their descendants living in the small villages on the other side of the city, but most of them are long gone."

"That's not fair," said Dayven indignantly. "The wizards may have meddled, but they exposed the handmaidens' cheating. They did the right thing!"

Reddick shrugged. "We did the right thing back at the lake, when we cut those peasants loose, but do you think the guards who report it are going to be fair?"

Dayven was silent.

"In any case," Reddick went on, "the Cenzar don't trust wizards. They won't let any of us stay in the city for long, and then only if someone vouches for our conduct."

"So we'll have to sneak in," Dayven concluded. "Most cities close their gates at sunset, and it will be almost dark by the time we get up there." He gazed up at the twisting road that was the only approach to the city gates. Anyone on it would be visible to the guards on the walls. "Wouldn't it be better not to call attention to ourselves by being the last ones through?"

"Good question." Reddick was digging in his pack. "You might as well get down. We're going to be here a while."

"And sneak through the gates in the morning." Dayven nodded, then led his horse over to join Reddick and began to unsaddle it. "Should we camp this close to the road? I know there's water here, but we could follow the stream to a safer place." They might admit wizards, but Dayven's scalp still prickled from being this close to the enemy's stronghold.

"Ah." Reddick pulled a bottle from his pack. "Let's have some wine and discuss it."

"You're joking. Not a mile from the Cenzar walls and you're going to get . . . you're going to drink?"

"No, I'm going to get drunk." The wizard uncorked the bottle and took a swig. "Courage from a jug. Haven't you heard of that?" He drank some more.

"You're not going to be in any shape to fool the guards tomorrow." Dayven eyed him grimly.

"Maybe you should meditate," Reddick told him. "You look a little upset."

"One of us has to make camp." Dayven unfastened his horse's bridle and looked for a place to tether it. "Besides, I hardly need to meditate to find power now."

"You're learning fast. You'll make a wizard yet." Reddick took a long pull at the bottle.

A puzzled frown tugged at Dayven's brows; in all the days they'd traveled together, this was the first time he'd seen his tutor drink. "How long do I have to study to be a wizard?" If he could keep a conversation going while the wizard became intoxicated he might learn something.

"It isn't a matter of how long, or even how much you know. It's a way of looking at things, how much you see and how you think. I suppose it's, well, perspective." Reddick chuckled foolishly. "When you start seein' five sides to a four-sided object, that's when you get the gray robe. That's why some wizards are young and some old men are still appren'ices."

"Why gray?" Dayven probed. "Why not white or black?" Had the wizard drunk enough to be loose-tongued? He seemed to be getting drunk awfully fast.

"Black's too hot in the sun." Reddick poured some of the wine on the front of his robe, capped the bottle and thrust it into his pack. "And white gets dirty too easy. Come on now." He mounted the mule. It took him several tries. "We mus' be going."

"Going where?" Surely he couldn't be that drunk? On just a few swallows?

"The city." His tutor blinked owlishly at him. "Where els'?" He wheeled the mule and started up the road at a canter.

"Wait! Reddick, stop!" Dayven spun for his own horse, but the animal wore neither saddle nor bridle and it would take too long to put them on. If Reddick encountered the Cenzar in this condition, anything might happen! Dayven turned and ran after his tutor on foot.

He could have caught the wizard if he hadn't been trying to keep out of sight of the city guards. Scrambling from one level of the road to the next, under the scant cover of brush and rock took time—too much time—curse the sot!

Struggling through the bushes in his long, tangling

robe, Dayven saw that his tutor had no qualms about being noticed. Trotting happily up the road in the gathering dark, he appeared to be singing.

Dayven was only about a hundred feet behind him when Reddick reached the great gate. It was closed. If the sot would be quiet for just a few minutes . . .

"Open up!" the wizard roared. He banged on the gate with his fist. "I demand admitshenshe . . . a'mishensh . . . I want in!"

Dayven sank into the bushes and swore. Reddick sounded more drunk than he had earlier.

Several torches were thrust through holes in the gate, illuminating the wizard, but leaving the top of the wall in shadow. *How efficient.* Dayven shivered.

"There are twelve arrows pointed at you, wizard." The Cenzar voice came from the wall above. "Get off the mule. Do nothing else. We've been watching you for some time. You and the shadow who tries so hard to conceal himself. Do nothing."

Dayven froze behind the screen of branches. They had spotted him, despite his care. Could they see him now? Was he out of arrow range? He thought not. He lowered himself to the ground, looking for some cover that arrows wouldn't pierce. There wasn't any. He wished he'd tried harder to learn the hiding spell.

". . . have come to visit the 'daffi Jeman." Reddick staggered as he came down from the saddle. He clung to it to hold himself upright. "I am his chief medical advishor. Must see 'im. 'Portant matter. He'll be very upset, you don' let me in."

A murmur of conversation arose on the wall, but Dayven couldn't hear what they said.

"What about your shadow? Does he also have an appointment with Endaffi Jeman?" It was a new voice, full of authority.

"Shadow?" Reddick looked around him. "Don't have a shadow, silly. S'almos' dark."

"I mean the person who followed you up the road."

"Oh, thas my 'prentice," said Reddick happily. "Be gentle when you pick him up, a'right? He's a bit . . ." He waved one finger vaguely in the direction of his temple. "A bit . . . you know." Dayven snarled silently.

The gate was opening. They were going to take Reddick into the city. Then they would come hunting for Dayven. He took a deep breath.

"Master!" he shouted. He rose slowly to his feet, flinching as the light found his body. No arrows flew. "Master, wait!"

Lifting his hands to show they were empty, Dayven ran to the wizard and flung himself against the broad back, burying his face in Reddick's robe, the perfect picture of a frightened simpleton.

The wizard reeked of wine. Dayven wanted to clench his fists and drive blows into the stocky body, but he didn't dare.

"Reddick?"

They had confined them in a guardhouse near the gate. Separate cells. They had searched them, taken Dayven's knife, said they would send for Endaffi Jeman in the morning, and gone.

"Reddick?" From the barred portal in his door, Dayven could see Reddick's cell. "Answer me, curse you, I know you can hear me!"

A faint snore came to his ears.

"Curse you!" Dayven pounded on the cell door. "Stupid sot." But he didn't believe it. Not anymore. They had entered the Cenzar city safely, without arousing a shadow of suspicion. An efficient man, this wizard. A formidable enemy.

Dayven sank down on the hard cot. He should rest. No doubt his devious companion would have them out of here shortly. And then he would discover just what the wizard was doing in the city of the enemy. It was a long time before Dayven fell asleep.

✧ ✧ ✧

He was awakened by the rattle of keys in the lock.

Reddick was grumbling his way down the hall, like a man with sousing sickness. At the guard's gesture, Dayven hurried after him.

They were released into the custody of a tall Cenzar, whose immaculate white robe made Dayven feel even more grubby. His features were narrower than most Tharns', and a trim black beard decorated his chin. His appearance was strange to Dayven's eyes, but the assurance of his manner was impossible to mistake.

". . . a good healer." Dayven heard only snatches of the reassuring murmur the tall Cenzar directed at the guard commander as they walked. "Endaffi Jeman will take full responsibility . . . old friends . . . no trouble I'm sure . . ."

Dayven wondered if a purse had changed hands. It wouldn't surprise him.

Reddick winced theatrically as they went out into the sunlight. Dayven remembered him doing the same thing the first time they met. Had his drunkenness been faked then as well? And if it was, who was he fooling then, and why? The warmth of the sun did nothing to alleviate the cold that crept through him. Dayven resolved to keep a close watch on his deceitful tutor.

Dayven's horse stood, saddled and waiting, with Reddick's mule and another horse. The guards must have gone down and found it. Dayven crushed down his gratitude. This was the enemy.

Reddick maintained a grumpy silence until they were out of the guard's sight. Then he turned to the tall man and a broad smile spread over his face.

"Ameen. I'd hoped to see you. How are you doing? How's your wife? That leg still giving her trouble?"

"All in my household are well, thanks to you, Master Reddick. The zondar is nearly empty today as there are horsemanship exercises in the field, but Endaffi Jeman remained behind. He is waiting for you."

"Good, he's just the man I want to see. Ameen, this is my apprentice, Dayven. Kid, Ameen is Endaffi Jeman's right hand. You want to stay on his good side."

Dayven nodded stiffly to the Cenzar. "May I ask a question? Who is Endaffi Jeman?" *And why did Reddick want to see him so badly?*

"He's head of the zondar, the warrior school where you'll spend the next couple of weeks. Remember? We talked about it. I'll settle it when I talk to Jeman. After that . . . We'll see. I'm going to be too busy here to spare much time for teaching you, I'm sorry, but there are other things I have to do."

"You mean you're just going to leave me at the zondar?" Dayven's heart sank. The thought of being abandoned among his enemies was bad enough, but if he was trapped in this zondar, how could he learn Reddick's true intentions. "Alone?"

"You will be most welcome in our school," Ameen put in kindly.

"You'll be all right. Trust me," said Riddick.

As if anyone could trust a wizard.

Reddick turned to Ameen and began asking about people he had healed. It sounded as if Reddick, and other wizards, visited the city regularly to work their healing magic, despite the Cenzars' distrust. The Tharn tolerated them for the same reason. Dayven let his horse fall behind and brooded. Even Reddick admitted that wizards were meddlers. The Cenzar were right not to trust them, and so was Lord Enar, even if sometimes they might do good. But how could he spy on Reddick if he wasn't with him? Dayven tried to think of some way to stay with the wizard, but the sights kept distracting him.

The streets teemed with people, and with the people came color—enough color to leave Dayven staring. The Tharn wore tastefully subdued shades. Peasants generally wore deeply dyed fabric that would survive many washings, but these people . . . A man carrying a basket of honking geese caught Dayven's eye—could he possibly believe a purple tunic over a butter-yellow shirt and scarlet pants became him? Everyone they passed looked like a festival performer. Their bright, flowing clothes and dark faces made Dayven feel increasingly conspicuous in his plain brown robe, but none of the Cenzar paid them any attention as Ameen guided Dayven and his tutor through their midst. Dayven remembered hearing that the Cenzar thought it rude to stare.

He rode up behind Reddick, and seized on a lull in the conversation. "Why is everyone dressed like . . . like . . ."

"Like Cenzar?" The question stung.

"But the Cenzar peasants in the valley don't wear colors like that!"

Reddick's brows rose, but his voice was mild. "They do on festival days. People always wear better clothes in a city. We look drab to them."

The idea of considering anything from a Cenzar point of view silenced Dayven. He fell back, staring at the bustling crowd, but eventually he was able to look past the people to the city itself. The houses looked like those in the Town-within-the-Walls, but they were roofed with slate instead of wooden shingles. Dayven could see that slate would last longer than wood, but how could the roof and walls support the weight of all that stone?

When the others rode through a wide gate into a tree-lined courtyard Dayven was watching a workman who was balancing two stone blocks on his head and almost rode past them.

Reddick rode to the steps that led to the door of the central tower and dismounted, looking around.

Ameen dismounted too and spread his hands expressively. "Alas, the stablemen have gone to watch the exercises. You know how it is; any excuse for a holiday. Will you wait while I stable your beasts? Then I will be pleased to announce you to the Endaffi."

"Don't worry about that." Reddick tossed his reins to Dayven. "The kid'll take care of the animals."

"If you would be so kind?" Ameen gestured to a low building. "The stable is there. You may choose any empty stalls. I'm sure you'll find all you need. We will be in the north corner of the main building on the highest floor, if you wish to join us when you're finished."

"Fine," Dayven muttered.

Ameen and Reddick vanished through the main

door. Dayven turned and led the horse and mule to the stable.

The wizard escaped him this easily. But it would have been out of his role to refuse to take the horses. It was going to be hard enough to spy on Reddick from a school—it would be impossible from a cell. He would have to pretend to accept the wizard's plan, at least for now.

The stable door hung open a crack. Dayven pushed through it and a bucket fell over his head. Something thick and sticky ran over his face, behind his ears, and down his robe. Dayven gasped and honey filled his mouth. He reached up and yanked off the bucket, swiping at his eyes. An explosion of color burst in his face. He flinched, but the explosion had no force. He looked down at himself. He was covered with honey and flower petals.

"A sweeter fate than you deserve after the way you used your spurs yesterday, you foul . . . Oh Lady!"

Dayven wiped his eyes again. A green and sky-blue blur resolved itself into a slim youth, about his own age, with curly black hair and a mobile face, which at the moment expressed surprise and dismay.

"You're not Rustaf," said the youth.

"No," said Dayven. "You half-baked, lame-brained, sorry-excuse-for-a-jackass, I'm not."

"I don't blame you for being angry," said the stranger apologetically. "I was expecting someone else. I knew he was planning to sneak away from the exercises and ride out to visit his lady friend." The youth was trying to keep his face straight, but the corners of his mouth kept twitching. Dayven's hands clenched into fists.

"I really am sorry," he finished. "My name is Vadeen." His fingers formed a polite steeple.

It would be stupid for a spy in enemy territory to offend people. Dayven lifted his hands, awkwardly returning the unaccustomed gesture. They were covered with petals.

Vadeen burst out laughing.

Dayven lost his temper. His leap knocked Vadeen to the floor; they rolled together in the straw, grappling and pummeling each other. Vadeen was taller, but he was handicapped by fits of laughter.

Dayven was on top, swinging wildly, when a hand closed over his collar and hauled him to his feet.

"What the——" Reddick stared at his disheveled apprentice. "Oh. I see." His mouth twitched.

All the frustration of dealing with the wizard, of the whole impossible situation, boiled up. Dayven swung a fist at Reddick, but his tutor caught it before the blow could connect.

"None of that now." Reddick turned to Vadeen.

The Cenzar boy, held fast in Ameen's grip, was almost as sticky and dirty as Dayven. A scrape along one of his cheekbones was beginning to darken. He had been laughing too hard to hurt Dayven.

"Well, kid, since you're now a student in the zondar, I guess you and this scoundrel are Jeman's problem." Reddick looked Dayven up and down and his lips twitched again. "It's not the way I'd dress to meet the head of the school, but it is . . . colorful."

Vadeen laughed.

Endaffi Jeman, who greeted Dayven with politely steepled fingers, did not laugh. Dayven was so grateful for it, he had to crush down an impulse to bow in return. A Guardian did not bow to his enemies. Still, he had to fight a ridiculous desire to cling to Reddick as the wizard introduced him to the Endaffi and departed. And that was ridiculous, for Reddick was as much his enemy as the Cenzar! Though the wizard did seem to have left Dayven in capable hands.

Perhaps the austere richness of the Endaffi's office had something to do with this feeling of nervous respect. Who'd have thought people who dressed so gaudily would appreciate unadorned wood? The intricate carving of the shutters and desk surpassed anything Dayven had ever seen. Lord Enar had nothing so fine, and this man was what, a schoolmaster? Perhaps that was the Cenzar equivalent of a bard. For it wasn't merely the setting, Dayven realized as the Cenzar boy recounted their story; the Endaffi, whose clothing was almost as restrained as a Tharn's, would command respect in a back alley wearing beggar's rags. Even that cocksure idiot, Vadeen, seemed a little . . . quelled. Somewhat to Dayven's surprise, the boy told the complete truth.

"So you see, Endaffi," Vadeen concluded, "the wizard's apprentice walked into a snare set for another. No one could blame him for his rage, especially when I laughed." He laughed again, remembering, but soon fell silent under the Endaffi's cool eyes.

"Dayven," Endaffi Jeman turned to him, "do you have anything to add to Vadeen's account of this lamentable incident."

"No, Endaffi. He told you everything."

"Vadeen always confesses," said the Endaffi dryly. "It is only unfortunate that he has to do it so often. But that is nothing to do with you. You have, in fact, been the victim of a grave fault in our hospitality. I offer you profound apologies on the behalf of the zondar and of the Cenzar people. Vadeen, no doubt, will offer his own apologies eventually." He steepled his fingers again and bowed slightly.

"He already did." Dayven found himself bowing in return. He had expected to be punished, not apologized to. The Endaffi must have read his face.

"In view of the provocation you received, your punishment will be light. For the future I warn you; brawling is not allowed."

He turned back to Vadeen.

"I suppose you, as usual, aren't the least bit sorry."

"Well, I'm sorry I got the wrong one, but aside from that, no, Endaffi."

Endaffi Jeman sighed. "Then it must be my job to make you sorry.

"First, as punishment for your breach of hospitality, you will be Dayven's companion for as long as he is here. He was a Tharn Watcherlad, but his people rejected him when he chose wizardry. He and his master are my guests in the city. Explain our ways to him, and keep him from trouble."

It was, Dayven supposed, the polite way of assigning Vadeen to guard him. He was glad he didn't need to spy on anyone but Reddick.

"Next, as punishment for sneaking away from your exercises, you are forbidden to take part in exercises yourself for a week. You are, however, required to attend and help Dayven, who will take your place. You will also spend two hours after dinner each evening assisting the cook."

Vadeen grimaced. "Yes, Endaffi."

"Finally, as punishment for the trick you planned to play on Rustaf—"

"But Endaffi, he—"

The Endaffi held up his hand for silence. "I know you think he misused one of the horses. I also know that to you there is no greater crime and that you felt justified in what you planned. But Vadeen, the decision was not yours. If you see a man misuse a horse you report it to the master-of-horse. You do not humiliate him personally. Nor do you take a switch to him, as you did last time."

Vadeen's eyes fell. "Yes, Endaffi."

"As I was saying, your punishment for this is to be banned from the stables until Rustaf returns. He has just left on an errand for me and will not be back for several weeks. If you are not allowed in the stables, perhaps he will find no unpleasant surprises awaiting him when he returns."

"But Endaffi, Nikkar is due to foal any day. It's going to be a difficult birth, too. If I am forbidden the stables, how can I—"

"Nikkar's foaling is the master-of-horse's business, not yours. I'm sure he can handle it without you.

"And now, Dayven." The Endaffi turned back to him. "You are permitted to move freely in our city only because Vadeen will accompany you at all times, and because I have taken responsibility for your actions. Don't thank me, for in return I am shifting the responsibility for Vadeen's behavior on to you. See that he does as I have said, and keep him out of further trouble. I will hold you accountable, at least in part, for his conduct.

"Vadeen, since you have missed the exercises, you may spend the rest of the day showing Dayven our city. The cook will expect you in the kitchen tonight."

"But Endaffi, Nikkar is—"

"That is all. You may go."

102

Dayven grabbed Vadeen's arm and pulled him out the door before his impudent tongue could get them in more trouble.

"And, Vadeen," the Endaffi called after them, "start your tour with the public bath. You both need it."

CHAPTER EIGHT

DAMISHAFF, THE CITY of the Cenzar, amazed and delighted Dayven in spite of himself.

After he exclaimed over the vaulted ceiling of the bathhouse, Vadeen took him to the Church of the Lady, and then fidgeted while Dayven stared at the stone arches soaring overhead. The low moaning that twined among them was oddly familiar.

"Wind pipes," Vadeen told him. "The Lady's voice."

Dayven stared at him, trying to ignore the combination of orange tunic and wine-colored britches. "But if you know it's just wind . . . ah, I mean, it doesn't sound much like a voice to me."

Vadeen smiled, but his eyes were serious. "It doesn't sound like a *human* voice, but it is made by the Lady's breath, which all life breathes back to her."

"I see," said Dayven. Actually he didn't, but the

church was even more beautiful than the Bardic Hall back home, and the spooky moaning almost made it seem alive, breathing. Perhaps he did see.

And were the Tharn and the Cenzar really so different? According to Vadeen, the Lady's handmaidens used the church to teach about how the Lady gifted the world with life, just as the bards in the Bardic Hall sung the history of the Tharn, and explained the workings of destiny. Of course, the bards also taught that the Cenzar goddess was only a peasant superstition. Still . . . If the Cenzar, in their gaudy colors, thought the Tharn looked drab, what might they think of the Tharns' beliefs about destiny?

As the next four days went by, Dayven found other things he liked about the city: the sweet and spicy fikka tarts they bought in stalls in the bazaar, the shaded gardens behind high walls, the politeness of the people he met. Even the warriors, who tried to teach him Cenzar fighting methods, were courteous—some even friendly.

Dayven found the Cenzar fighting style very different from his own. Their armor was lighter than the Tharns' heavy plate and they wore much less of it— sometimes no more than a breastplate and bracers to protect their arms. Dayven thought that was unbelievably reckless, until he saw their exercises. They relied on their ability to dodge and duck to protect themselves. And their horses, which were wonderfully well trained, could easily carry them out of reach of an enemy's weapon. Dayven was proud to learn that on foot he could usually hold his own with a sword—at least against boys near his own age. But the moment they all mounted horses, the Cenzar had him hopelessly overmatched. Watching those horses twist and spin, and remembering how much all that armor slowed a man down, Dayven became very thoughtful.

His mission was to spy on Reddick, but the task Reddick had given him, to observe the Cenzar's fighting methods, was beginning to seem every bit as valuable. Could the wizard be innocent after all? Even if he wasn't, Dayven couldn't think of any way to spy on him. He'd seen Reddick in the zondar a few times, talking to the teachers, but he didn't know what they were talking about, and he couldn't think of any reason to ask.

There were also Cenzar customs that Dayven didn't like. At his first dinner, as dish after dish of vegetables and grain passed by, he almost insulted the Cenzar by asking where the meat was. Only a few shreds of fowl were served—this was a poor man's table! But the

Cenzar were not poor; this must be the diet they preferred. At least it accounted for the absence of forks; there was nothing on the table worth spearing. Dayven, having no desire to anger his hosts, kept his comments to himself, but he hungered for a thick slab of beef or lamb or even goat.

When they were not at lessons, Vadeen showed Dayven different parts of the city. It was in the street of the spice sellers, on his fifth day in Damishaff, that he saw Reddick talking to a richly dressed old man.

Dayven grabbed Vadeen's arm and pulled him around a corner.

"What did you do that for?"

"My tutor's out there," Dayven whispered. He peered around the corner and ducked back. "He's talking to a man."

"Why shouldn't he? You don't want him to see you?"

"I don't . . . ah, we had a fight." He hoped Vadeen wouldn't ask what the fight was about—or when it had taken place. He hadn't spoken to Reddick since the wizard left him at the zondar. "Can you tell me who he's with?"

Vadeen looked. "That's Mirin, the apothecary. He was a wizard's apprentice himself, I heard. But he never became a wizard, or they wouldn't have let him stay here. Is there some reason he shouldn't talk to your master?"

"No, of course not." Dayven peeked again. Reddick and the apothecary were still there. "Let's go this way, Vadeen. I want . . . I want to see the church again." The Cenzar boy eyed him suspiciously, but allowed himself to be led in the opposite direction without protest.

"I don't know why Mirin never became a wizard," Vadeen commented. "I heard he studied with them for many years. Is it so hard to become a wizard?"

"He probably couldn't see the fifth side," said Dayven absently. He was grateful for Vadeen's tact. He didn't want Reddick to catch his apprentice spying on him. Of course, he *should* have been spying on him for the last five days.

"Why do wizards wear gray?" asked Vadeen curiously. "I know that your people don't share the love of color, with which the Lady has gifted us, and I can understand that with their uncertain reputation wizards might not want to wear black, but why not some pleasing color?"

"Gets dirty too easy," said Dayven absently. He didn't even know where Reddick was staying. He should sneak out tonight and try to find him. During the day, despite his casual attitude, Vadeen was careful not to let Dayven wander off alone, but Dayven thought that was as much to keep him safe as to spy on him. They had moved a bed into Vadeen's room for Dayven, so they slept together, but in the evening, within the zondar's walls, Vadeen let him do as he pleased. There was a watchman at the zondar's gates, but that was just an excuse; the truth was that Dayven hadn't quite dared to go wandering alone in an enemy city. If he waited till after kitchen duty, it would be easy enough for him to escape over the zondar's wall . . . because Vadeen trusted him. *A Guardian should be worthy of trust—the fifth rule.*

But to be worthy of Vadeen's trust, he would have to betray Lord Enar's—and it was to Lord Enar that had promised his loyalty, not to Vadeen. Certainly not to Reddick!

Vadeen saw that Dayven was troubled and changed the subject with typical Cenzar courtesy. Even though he was an enemy Tharn, everyone treated him hospitably, because he was a guest in their city. Well, almost everyone.

"The Tharn are superstitious barbarians, without manners or courage. Once we have beaten their army into the mud they will pack up and move on. Tharns never hold anything long. That's why they never build anything." The cook scratched his dirty turquoise shirt and glared at Vadeen, who stopped scrubbing bowls and turned to wink sympathetically at Dayven. It had taken only one evening with the cook to turn the two boys into allies.

"We've stayed in the Town-within-the-Walls for three generations," Dayven, who was drying, declared proudly. "We've beaten your army before, and we'll do it again."

"After you stole the land in the first place by a foul trick, inviting our generals to meet and dine with you in peace and then attacking them as they ate."

Dayven blushed. The Tharn version of the story referred to this as "the Lordowner's wise plan," but no one bragged about it. Soren had once called it a despicable way to win.

"Well, you're wrong about us not staying," he told the cook. "Before, we kept moving because we were looking for this valley. Now it's found, we'll never have to move on again."

The cook snorted, but Vadeen looked curious. "What do you mean, you were looking for this valley?"

"It was a prophecy," Dayven explained. His voice

110

slid into the cadence of the bard as he recited the words that had consoled and motivated so many generations of his ancestors. "Long ago there was a great bard, Geordic, who had the seer's gift. When our ancestors were driven from their homeland, he foresaw our people's destiny. He said we would be forced to roam for many generations, but that someday we would come to a valley, even more lovely and fertile than the land we lost, and there we would remain."

The cook sniggered. "Did this seer also say you would have to steal the land by treachery and—"

"It isn't the treachery he minds," said Vadeen from his place by the washtub. "It's that the meal was inter-rupted. That's all cooks care about."

"You keep scrubbing, dung-shoveler." The cook aimed a cuff at Vadeen, but the Cenzar boy ducked it easily, being familiar with the cook's habits.

"I'm a *rashief*, a mounted warrior, not a dung-shoveler," Vadeen protested.

"Oh, a rashief, are you? What great races have you ridden? What battles have you fought, to deserve that title?"

"None yet," said Vadeen. "But I will. Already I know much. Take Nikkar for instance. The master-of-horse, who knows more about horses than any warrior could, says she's going to foal in two weeks—but it's going to be much sooner than that. I can tell by the way she acts. That is the knowledge of a true rashief."

"But for now you are a dung-shoveler who befriends the enemy that is draining the life from our land."

"Dayven is a wizard," said Vadeen. "Wizards revere life."

"That's all they revere. Not only are they godless infidels, but they serve no lord. Men without faith or loyalty are less than animals."

"At least we bathe oftener than animals do," said Dayven smartly. "Which is more than I can say for some." His direct glance left no doubt who he meant and Vadeen snickered.

Actually, most Cenzar bathed more often than the Tharn did. Vadeen had taken him to the baths almost daily. Dayven was sure it couldn't be good for his skin, but none of the Cenzar seemed to suffer from it.

Sometimes in the bazaar, Dayven saw a bargainer look straight at someone and pinch their nostrils shut; the gesture's meaning was so plain he didn't need to ask Vadeen for a translation. Perhaps it wasn't considered polite to say it plainly. Dayven thought he was getting a grip on how Cenzar manners worked.

The cook's round face turned red. "You are fine

ones to speak of cleanliness. You haven't even started the plates yet."

He tipped the towering stack of dishes into the washbasin and a sheet of dirty water drenched both boys. "Yes, you are fine ones to talk of cleanliness. You'd better have those shining when I get back."

He strolled out of the kitchen, chuckling at the sharpness of his own wit.

"Cenzar snake-dung," muttered Dayven, dabbing at his damp robe with the drying cloth.

Vadeen was even wetter. He took off his soaked apron, threw it on the floor, and folded his arms.

"Don't let it bother you," he said majestically. "That potbellied pot-scrubber is as the dust beneath our feet. We will transcend his insults."

"What do you mean? That we should forget it?"

"Not at all," said Vadeen. "We should get even."

The cook awakened to the sound of Ameen's whistle. The master-of-the-household used it to summon servants who might be scattered throughout the school. But in his kitchen at this hour of the morning it could mean only one thing: a surprise inspection. The cook yawned. It was a nuisance, but it didn't matter. He had checked the kitchen before he went to bed. Those lazy

113

boys had done a decent job.

He rolled out of bed and stepped into his pants. Or tried to. The right leg went on fine, but he couldn't put his foot through the left one.

The whistle sounded again, a little louder. Ameen was a busy man. He expected people to come when summoned.

The cook thrust his foot into his trousers and gasped as he heard the cloth around the ankle rip. He stared at the dangling threads; the ankle had been sewn shut!

The whistle sounded again.

The cook grabbed his shirt, pulled it on, and discovered the buttons were missing. Vadeen and the Tharn brat. Wait till he got his hands on them; they'd see who laughed last!

The whistle again, shrill and impatient.

Oh well. Ameen never cared how he looked, as long as the kitchen was clean and the food good.

The cook put on his slippers. He wasn't surprised when the heels came loose, flapping noisily with every step he took.

Feeling like he was wading through a nightmare, the cook flapped hurriedly down the stairs.

Morning sun streamed through the open doorway,

silhouetting Ameen's white-clad figure and lighting the chaos and filth of the kitchen.

The cook's jaw dropped. It had been tidy, if not spotless, when he went to bed, but now . . .

Every pot was dirty, even those jumbled in the half open cupboards. A broken egg decorated the floor at Ameen's feet and eggy footprints tracked through spilled flour. Grease and rotting vegetables were everywhere.

The cook began to babble. It was a plot, a dastardly plot to disgrace him in the eyes of the esteemed master-of-the-household, may the Lady strike him mute if he lied. The cook wrung his hands, blinking in the brilliant light at Ameen's still form.

Ameen said nothing.

The cook begged his excellency for one more chance. The cook would catch the ones who had committed this outrage in his kitchen and wring the truth from them. Ameen said nothing.

The cook fell to his knees and bowed to the ground. The cook spoke of his aged mother who depended on his salary and would be thrown into the street to starve if he had no job. The cook heard a whoop of stifled laughter and looked up sharply. His eyes finally adjusted to the light.

Ameen said nothing. Ameen couldn't say anything, because Ameen wasn't there.

With a snarl of rage the cook reached up and tore the white-clad dummy from the threads that suspended it in the doorway.

Shrieking with laughter, Dayven and Vadeen burst from their hiding place and raced for the street. Snatching up a knife, the cook followed.

CHAPTER NINE

"I THINK HE'S GAINING," Dayven puffed. "Who'd have thought . . . he'd chase us this far?"

"He's pretty mad," Vadeen agreed, sprinting along beside him. "When we get to the next alley . . . you go in. I'll lead him into . . . bazaar and lose him. Meet me back at the zondar. We'll talk to the Endaffi together. Goes easier on you . . . if you confess first."

"But what if—"

"Now!" Vadeen shoved him into an alley and ran on, down the street to the bazaar. "Hey, pudding gut!" Dayven heard him call. "Come on, potbelly, the race is to the swift!"

Dayven sprinted down the alley to a pile of grain bags and crouched behind them. The cook ran past the entrance. With a sigh of relief, Dayven turned to continue down the alley and out, but a high wall blocked his way. There was no way out. Dayven turned to run back to the street and saw the cook peer around the corner.

Heart hammering, he ducked behind the sacks and listened to the cook's footsteps come down the alley.

Why had he let Vadeen talk him into this? His best hope was to hide. In the dim light his robe might be mistaken for one of the sacks—by a man three-quarters blind. The footsteps came closer.

I am not here, said Dayven desperately, in the silence of his mind. He pulled his hood over his head and leaned into the pile of sacks, feeling the roughness of the cloth against his face. He reached out and felt it with his thoughts, with his power.

I am part of the sack. I am covered by it. Dayven built a shield of power in his mind. It looked like a sack. Cowering behind it, he melted himself into the pile of grain.

The footsteps walked past him. A furious curse from the end of the alley made him risk a glance. The cook was glaring at a board that leaned against the wall. Dayven might have used it to climb over, if he'd had time.

The cook turned and stamped out of the alley, cursing

under his breath. Dayven saw the knife and hid his face again, but the cook passed him without hesitation.

Dayven waited several minutes before he let the shield of power fade. Standing, he looked at the grain sacks and then at his robe. They didn't look at all alike.

He stared at the sacks for a long time; then he went back to the zondar to find Vadeen.

Vadeen was nowhere to be found. By midafternoon Dayven was so worried he went to Endaffi Jeman.

"The cook had a knife," he finished his long explanation. His palms were damp and he wiped them on his robe. "If he went on to the bazaar, he might have caught Vadeen and . . . and . . ."

"If you're trying to suggest that Vadeen is likely to appear in the stew this evening," said the Endaffi dryly, "allow me to set your mind at ease. Our unfortunate cook has been the victim of many student pranks, and yes, has even chased his tormentors with a knife, but I assure you, whatever the provocation, he won't use it."

"Then where's Vadeen?"

"I have no idea," said the Endaffi. "But since I made you responsible for keeping him out of trouble, I suggest you find him and bring him to me. To speed your search, let me point out that the longer I wait, the

119

longer I'll have to think up an appropriate punishment for you both."

Dayven swallowed. "I'll find him, Endaffi."

"I would if I were you," said the Endaffi. "Soon."

The sun was setting and Vadeen was still missing. Dayven had looked everywhere Vadeen had taken him in Damishaff. Now he slumped on his bed in their room, defeated, cradling his cocoon in his hands.

It was comforting to stretch his mind out to that small spark of life. It was transforming itself, but he couldn't tell how; he could only sense the existence of the change. He wished, with an intensity that frightened him, that he could know it completely.

He hadn't found Reddick today either. The preparations for their prank had interfered with Dayven's plan to follow the wizard last night. What was his tutor doing now? An idea sprang into his mind. He had considered using scrying to spy on Reddick, but he feared that the wizard might be able to sense it. Could he find Vadeen that way? Dayven closed his eyes and thought about Vadeen. Then he released the power so it welled slowly through his being and concentrated on Vadeen with all his might.

Nothing happened.

120

Had he done it wrong? Frowning faintly, Dayven thought of Soren instead. The vision formed instantly.

Soren was sitting on his bed, polishing a breastplate. The rest of the armor was scattered on the floor at his feet; it looked new. Then Soren reached for the polish pot, and the sun flashed on the silver whistle hanging around his neck.

Soren had made Guardian! He would lead a troop in the coming battle, and Dayven could ride with him as his Watcherlad. They had planned it that way, just weeks ago, but now Dayven felt only distant pleasure at the prospect, not blazing excitement—as if it was someone else's destiny and he was just a spectator. Cold twisted his guts.

"Hey." Someone shook his shoulder gently and the vision faded. Dayven looked up into Reddick's worried face. "You'd better not make a habit of that, kid. It's not polite to watch people when they don't know you're there. I didn't know you knew how."

Hugging himself against the lingering chill of fear, Dayven explained, quickly, and then explained why it was so urgent that he find Vadeen. "I don't understand why I can't see him at all, when I see Soren so easily."

"That's simple. You don't know Vadeen as well as you know Soren."

"I do know Vadeen," Dayven protested. "I was with him just this morning."

"But do you know his essence?" Reddick asked. "His inner being that makes him different from everyone else in the world?"

"I guess not."

"That's what you need in order to scry for someone. Unless you can distinguish their essence, you haven't got a chance."

"Then you couldn't find Vadeen for me?"

"Nope." Reddick shook his head. "Only great wizards can scry for someone they don't know. Sometimes the greatest can even scry someone's future, though it's not very reliable. But it does invade people's privacy, so you should watch how you use it. I'm not saying you were wrong this time, but in the future be careful—it's an easy gift to abuse."

"I wasn't trying to spy on him," said Dayven indignantly. "Besides, I thought wizards didn't have any rules."

"It's not about rules," said Reddick. "It's about thinking things through before you act. Don't you ever do things you wouldn't want someone else to see? Not because they're wrong, just because they're private?"

122

"Of course. Everyone does."

"Exactly," said Reddick. "But you don't have to worry about getting in trouble for not finding Vadeen, or for your stunt with the cook. That's what I came to tell you. We're leaving tomorrow."

Dayven's jaw dropped. "But we've only been here a few days! I—"

"You've had a chance to observe the Cenzar training. I've found out what I need to know about their army. I need to see one more person tonight, then we can go. Jeman will be there; I'll tell him you're no longer part of the zondar, so you can stop fretting." Reddick stood and turned toward the door.

They couldn't leave yet—Dayven had no idea what Reddick had done! *Stall for time. But what* . . . "But what about Vadeen? I have to send him to the Endaffi as soon as I can or he'll be in even more trouble."

"So figure out where he is," said Reddick. "You may not know his essence, but he's your friend. What would keep him from meeting you like he said he would? Just because you've got magic, doesn't mean you get to put your brain out to pasture."

Then he left. Left to finish his real mission, whatever it was. Dayven had thought they'd spend weeks in

Damishaff! He was sure Reddick said that, or at least implied it. Deliberately? He couldn't follow Reddick now without getting caught, but perhaps tonight he could sneak out—find this mysterious meeting, find out what that deceitful *wizard* had been up to.

Meanwhile, he had to find Vadeen. For a deceitful wizard, Reddick gave good advice. Once he thought about it, Dayven knew exactly where Vadeen would be.

CHAPTER TEN

"STEADY, NIKKAR. Steady, girl." Vadeen's voice soothing the laboring mare was the first thing Dayven heard in the deserted stable. He made his way toward the pool of light that surrounded the stall at one end.

"Vadeen," he called softly. "You have to come now. The Endaffi is furious."

"Dayven, where is the master-of-horse?" All Vadeen's attention was on the mare, who lay on her side, her glossy hide dark with sweat. Sweat stains marked Vadeen's brilliant gold shirt, and the smudges on his rolled-up sleeves looked like blood. "This is taking too long. The colt's twisted in the womb and can't come out. He'll have to be turned."

The mare's muscles contracted and she grunted, panting with pain and effort.

"I thought I should check on Nikkar before I went to meet you. I could tell the foal was coming. I looked for the master-of-horse, but I couldn't find him. He's not in the zondar. I sent the night-groom to look in town, but that was hours ago and he hasn't come back."

The mare grunted again, hooves thrashing in the straw.

Vadeen ran his hands over her swollen body. "We can't wait any longer," he said softly. "Hold her head, Dayven. Talk to her. Keep her quiet. I'm going to turn the colt."

So Dayven sat by the mare's head, gentling her with his voice and his hands, and watched his friend's sure movements until the tiny, slippery foal squirted into Vadeen's arms.

A rush of bright blood followed it.

Vadeen paled. "It's too much," he whispered. "I know it's too much."

Another rush of blood dyed the straw and soaked the mare's tail.

"She's bleeding inside. Oh Lady, I don't know what to do. I waited too long. Where is the master-of-horse!"

Dayven stroked down the mare's damp neck and over her shoulders to her belly. She was quiet now, ominously quiet.

To guard and defend those weaker than himself was a Guardian's first rule—surely that included this weary creature? Magic flowed through Dayven's hands. His mind found the torn flesh inside her and he willed his power to work, feeling the blood loss slow as the mare's weary body found its way back to wholeness.

When the job was finished he opened his eyes and gave the mare a final pat.

Vadeen stared at him in awe. "Thank you," he whispered. "I never wanted to be anything but a rashief. But I see now that it must be wonderful to be a wizard, too."

"It is," said Dayven. "It *would* be." The joy of it cut like a knife—renouncing that joy would be the hardest test. But at least he hadn't altered anyone's destiny with magic. Except, perhaps, his own.

"What do you mean? What's wrong?"

The mare stood shakily and nuzzled the shivering foal.

"Come," said Vadeen, taking Dayven's arm and pulling him from the stall. "They'll be better alone now."

They watched through the rails as the mare licked her foal dry. Vadeen waited patiently.

"I'm not going to be a wizard," Dayven finally confessed. "I promised my cousin I'd come back and become a Guardian once I'd . . . ah . . ."

"Observed our fighting skills," Vadeen finished calmly.

"You know about that?"

"Of course. Your friend Reddick talked to the master-of-arms. He pointed out that it would give us a chance to learn about Tharn fighting skills as well."

"Fate curse him," said Dayven. "We were right not to trust him. And I've failed."

"How?"

"Learning about your fighting techniques was only part of what I was supposed to do," Dayven told him furiously. "The other part was to keep an eye on Reddick. Lord Enar doesn't trust the wizards."

"He'd be a fool if he did. I don't mean to insult you, but the wizards . . . No one trusts them. If I were your Lord Enar, and was sending a wizard to the enemy camp, I'd send someone to watch him. But are you sure the wizards are helping us? They've been allowed to visit our city, to do healing here, for nearly a century, but they've never helped us fight before. If they were doing it now surely there'd be rumors, and if there were a rumor, I'd hear it. Besides, who'd choose Reddick for such a mission?"

"What do you mean?"

Vadeen shrugged. "I like your tutor, Dayven, but . . . He's been in the city before. He . . . well, he isn't a very sober person. I'm sure your people have nothing to fear from him."

Dayven decided that his doubts about Reddick's drinking were too complicated to explain. "Maybe we don't, but I was supposed to find out for sure. And I've failed," Dayven repeated bitterly. "We're leaving tomorrow. He's at his last meeting right now. I have no idea what he's been doing and no time to find out."

"There is tonight. Do you know where this meeting is?" Vadeen's eyes sparkled with mischief—an all-too-familiar expression. It set hope and dread warring in Dayven's heart.

"No," said Dayven. "I thought about that, but all I know it that Endaffi Jeman's going to be there."

"Then they're probably in the Endaffi's private study. I know just how to spy on it; I have frequently had to concern myself with what was said in the Endaffi's study."

Dayven stared at his friend. "You'd help me spy on your own people?"

Vadeen looked unusually serious. "If I thought you'd hear anything but gossip between old friends, I wouldn't. But I owe you for saving Nikkar, so we'll go

129

to this meeting and make certain that Reddick is not a conspirator. Then you can go home with your mission accomplished, and your mind at peace, and not get into trouble."

"That reminds me," said Dayven. "You're already in trouble. Just tell me where to go. I don't want you involved if I get caught."

"I," said Vadeen, with the return of his usual reckless good cheer, "am in so much trouble that it won't matter if I get caught. I might as well take advantage of it. I wouldn't have missed the look on the cook's face for the world. Come on, let me get cleaned up and I'll take you to the meeting."

With a slithering scrape, Dayven slid quietly down the shingles to kneel beside Vadeen. They had reached the roof from the top of a tree so high it made Dayven's palms clammy to remember it. Now, crawling down the roof edge after his friend, he managed to stay calm by the simple trick of never looking down.

Vadeen stopped and gestured below them. Reddick's voice came clearly from the open window beneath their feet.

". . . don't need to worry about the boy," he said.

"I've seen to it that he knows nothing of importance."

"But he was sent as a spy." It was a strange voice, deep and harsh. "He may have succeeded in learning more than you think. I say we kill him."

Dayven's knees went weak and he gripped the stone tighter, straining to hear.

"No chance," said Reddick firmly. "By the fates, Arrod, the kid's my apprentice! You—"

"If I might propose a compromise," Endaffi Jeman interrupted. "Dayven could stay in the zondar. We would keep him from escaping, but we would also keep him safe."

"No," said Reddick. "For one thing, most of the zondar will be in the war. Besides, he has to come back with me. Haven't you been listening? He was sent to spy on me as much as on you—maybe more. If I come back without him they won't believe a word I say. And my convincing Enar to bring his army out from behind the walls and fight you on the plain is the best chance you have of winning."

Dayven gasped.

"What was that?" said the one they called Arrod. Chairs scraped across the floor, and Dayven's heart lurched into his throat. As their footsteps neared the window, he and Vadeen flattened against the stone. Dayven found himself covered with a shield of power; he'd thrown it up without even thinking about it.

"I don't see anything." It was Reddick, right below them.

"Gentlemen," said the Endaffi. "I assure you it is impossible to overhear a conversation in this room. The walls are more than a foot thick and we are five stories from the ground. If the guard outside the door was overpowered we would hear it."

Dayven felt the familiar tingle of magic being used and a wave of power brushed the surface of his shield. He sank his mind into the stone beneath him and blanked his thoughts. The searching touch did not return.

"What about the roof?" Arrod asked.

"General, a mountain goat would have trouble climbing to that roof. Perhaps it was a bird you heard. In any case, I think Reddick is right. If he is to be believed, Dayven must return with him."

"And if the boy says he's not to be trusted, what then?"

"Then they'll hang me," said Reddick cheerfully. "And possibly all the other wizards as well, and you'll end up besieging the city, which is just what you'd have to do if I wasn't involved."

"Even if you fail, wizard, we will win," said Arrod. "We may not be able to breach Miskafar's walls, but we can starve them out. We've prepared for this for a long time—we have supplies for almost a year. With your harvest not yet in, supplies in your city will be low. The Tharn are no longer the only ones with steel weapons. Our time has come."

"Maybe," said Reddick dryly. "But you've besieged the city before, and Miskafar has never fallen."

"That was before the land began to die. Your harvests have been growing less for many years now. You're not as well supplied as you were a generation ago. This time we will win. Soon, it would be too late to matter."

"I know that," said Reddick. "But we both know your best chance to win quickly, with the least loss of life, is to meet the Tharn troops in the great plain and simply out-fight them. The wizards can help you there, too. We'll cast spells on the Tharns' weapons and equipment so it will break or fail them."

"And how will we know, wizard, whether Enar trusted you enough that we will be granted all this aid?"

"Simple," said Reddick. "If the Tharn army is out on

the plain waiting for you, then I succeeded. If they're shut up inside the city, you're on your own." There was a long pause.

"He's right, Arrod," said the Endaffi. "You aren't required to trust him. The results of his actions will show themselves when we reach the plain. Gentlemen, there seems to be little else to be said. Would you care for some wine before you leave?"

No one wanted wine. The chairs scraped again and the men left the room. Vadeen had to reach out and pull Dayven's sleeve to make him crawl after him. The climb down should have been terrifying, but Dayven barely noticed it.

Neither spoke until they were back in their room. The flame quivered in Vadeen's hands as he lit the lamp. "What are you going to do?" he asked quietly.

"I don't know," said Dayven. He felt numb, as if a blow had struck him but not yet begun to hurt. "It's hard to believe that Reddick . . . I hadn't realized how much I liked him." Even the wizard's annoying habit of calling him "kid" had started to seem familiar. "What are *you* going to do?"

He had never seen Vadeen look so serious.

"I must stop you from leaving. But if I tell them

what we learned, Arrod will want to kill you. The Endaffi would try to protect you, but General Arrod is powerful."

Dayven was silent.

"And your wizard is right. Lord Enar won't believe him if you aren't there to confirm what he says."

Of course, Vadeen wanted Reddick's plot to succeed. But . . .

"What happens," Dayven asked, "if I tell Lord Enar everything we heard tonight?"

Vadeen did not meet his eyes. "Then we besiege Miskafar. The outcome of a battle is in the Lady's hands; if she wishes us to win then we will, if not, we won't. You would say it is destiny, and already decided. Either way, nothing you do will make much difference. It would go hard with your wizard though." He began to pace. "Would you betray him? Your people will kill him, Dayven."

"I have to." The control that kept Dayven's voice steady made it sound cold, but there was nothing he could do about that. His hand crept into the folds of his robe and closed over the clay pot that held the cocoon. It wasn't much larger than his fist, for the wizards' healing salves were used in small doses, but the clay was thick and heavy. The thought of using it as a weapon made his stomach twist. "As you'll have to betray me."

"But you're my friend!" Vadeen turned and paced toward him. "And you saved Nikkar. I owe you—"

As he turned to pace away, Dayven leapt forward and slammed the clay pot against the back of his head. Vadeen slumped to the floor. Dayven's magic reached the injured boy before his trembling hands did, sensing the rich shimmer of life. He clenched his teeth to keep them from chattering. At least there was no blood.

With a little concentration, he found the ache that radiated from the back of his friend's skull. There didn't seem to be any serious damage, thank the fates!

"I'm sorry," he said, shaking, staring down at Vadeen's sprawled body. He recognized the absurdity of apologizing to someone who couldn't hear him, but it didn't matter—he had to say it. His mind reached out to the cocoon; as always, it soothed him to sense the small life within it. At least there was something he hadn't hurt. His trembling began to still.

"I'm sorry," he said again as he rummaged through the room for some rope. "I'll heal your head as soon as you're tied up, I promise. It will be an uncomfortable night, but someone will find you after I'm gone. Try to understand. Please. It's a test of honor."

He found a strong cord and knelt beside Vadeen.

"I know what I have to do." He looped the cord over Vadeen's wrists. "But I never thought honor would feel like betrayal."

CHAPTER ELEVEN

THEY RODE OUT of the main gate at dawn. One of
the guards lifted steepled fingers to Reddick
and smiled. The sight infuriated Dayven,
quelling the horror he felt at the thought of his
tutor dying a traitor's death . . . for a few moments.
Honor used to seem so clear to him. Now it had faded
into shades of gray. Like a wizard's robe.

The road down the high cliffs that kept the Tharn
from conquering Damishaff was too difficult for conversation. They had three days' hard riding to do before
they reached the Town-within-the-Walls, and the sky
was heavy with clouds. The dismal weather matched
Dayven's mood so perfectly that they rode for most of
the day before he realized it wasn't just the promise of
rain and his own grim thoughts that were depressing
him. He reined in and looked around.

Two weeks ago he would have passed these fields and seen nothing amiss. Now, with wizard's eyes, he saw the scrawny seed heads, the thin stalks, the small signs of death. He realized he'd been riding past fields like this for hours.

Reddick pulled his mule around, watching Dayven thoughtfully.

"What's wrong with these crops?" the boy asked. "They're terrible."

"I thought you'd never ask," said Reddick. "The land is weakening. You've heard people say it before, I know."

Dayven remembered what the cook had said. "I thought it was just some Cenzar superstition. You know, the land grieving for its rightful masters."

"I don't think the land knows who owns it," said Reddick. "The problem is the way it's being farmed. The Tharn are new to this valley."

"We've been here for—"

"Three generations." His tutor nodded. "But the Cenzar have been farming this land for hundreds of generations. They know things about it the Tharn could never understand."

"Well, I don't understand."

"That's because this kind of thing isn't covered in the battle songs. When the Tharn lived in the northern forests they were a moving people. They'd build a city out of wood, farm the area they cleared to get the lumber, and graze their herds in the meadows. In twenty, maybe thirty years, the grazing would be gone and they'd move to another part of the forest and build a new city. The soil in the forest was rich; they never stayed in one place long enough to wear it out."

"Wear it out? Dirt can't wear out."

"Wrong. Like there are differences in rocks, there are differences in the earth. In this valley, there's less rain and the soil is sandy. That's why there's no forest. But the Cenzar raised rich harvests here, year after year. They had a system. Plant corn or barley in a field one year, and wheat the next. These crops wear the soil out. So you plant beans the next year. We don't know how, but beans refresh the earth. Then the fourth year you don't plant anything, just leave the field to rest. Next year you can plant corn or barley again and get a fine crop."

Dayven gazed over the fields around them. "These are all planted in wheat or corn or barley. I haven't seen any empty ones."

Reddick nodded. "When the Tharn conquered the valley, they didn't understand. Because they knew how to make steel, and the Cenzar didn't, they thought they knew more about everything. The Tharn were herdsmen; they called the farmers lazy when they saw that every fourth field was empty. And their herds needed grain.

"The farmers tried to explain, and later the wizards did too, but none of the Guardians would listen. So we found a man who did understand, and tried to put him in power. You know how that ended."

"Was *that* the cause of the wizards' rebellion?"

Reddick nodded grimly.

"My grandmother died in it," Dayven told him. "The wizard Adina. Didn't you know?" He had spent his life despising the woman for her treachery, for the disgrace she'd brought upon her family, but this . . . this was courage worthy of a Guardian!

"Why would I?" Reddick asked. "You thought we kept track of wizards' descendants? We don't. It really isn't hereditary; you have magic because of you, not your grandmother. You should be proud of her, though. She died for a good cause."

"So now . . . Ah, why did the wizards stay? After so many were killed, I'd think you'd have given up."

"That's the downside of being a wizard. Once you've

seen, really *seen* something like this, you can't turn your back on it. We had to stay, to keep trying. Now it's almost too late."

"What do you mean?"

"The land isn't just weakening—it's dying. Every year the crops are thinner. If we start now it could be brought back, made healthy again. But we have to start now. Another ten years, maybe as few as five, and the land will be past healing. In another generation nothing will grow in this valley. Not enough to feed men. And then—"

"The Tharn will move on," murmured Dayven. "Leaving famine and desolation behind them."

"You got it, kid."

The rain fell that evening. Crouched by the snapping fire, Dayven watched his tutor feed spices into the stew pot.

He hoped, without much confidence, that the greased, tight-woven blanket wrapped around him would keep water from soaking through. The rain didn't seem to bother Reddick at all.

"Cheer up. We've got fire, food, and the trees are keeping the worst of it off. I thought showing fortitude in adversity was Guardians' rule number . . . seven?"

"Eight. But I'm not a Guardian, am I?" *If he revealed the wizard's plan, Lord Enar would probably make him one. The thought did nothing to cheer him.* "Not even a ghost would be out in this weather if it had any sense—which evidently wizards don't."

Reddick laughed. "No one's ever accused us of being sensible."

Dayven glared at him, and then thought of something. "Do all wizards become ghosts?"

"What?"

Dayven pulled the blanket tighter. "They say ghosts are people who lost their true path. So I wondered . . ."

Reddick settled himself comfortably. "All right, let's take this step by step. How do you know what your destiny is?"

"Those on their true path feel confident and certain," Dayven recited. "The false path brings doubt and dismay." He was definitely on a false path now. The problem was, he couldn't see any way to get off of it.

"So why would anyone follow a false path?"

"They're tempted by greed, or weakness when the true path becomes hard."

"Right. So how do you know the difference between

143

a true path that's hard and a false one?"

"Well . . ."

"Exactly."

Did that mean this terrible choice was his true destiny?
Dayven shivered. "It's easy for you, isn't it? Wizards
don't believe in anything."

"Not true, kid. We believe in lots of things—and
one of them is that it's choice, not destiny, that decides
our fate. Have you ever wondered exactly how wizards
alter men's destinies?"

"Well, I assumed . . ." Dayven fell silent. He had
always known that wizards lured men from their true
path, but how they went about it was something he'd
never considered before.

"Mostly, it's because we show them choices," said
Reddick quietly. "Choices their own people don't offer
them. Choices they might never even have thought of
before."

"And you think that's a good thing?" Dayven struggled to keep the betraying anger out of his voice.

"Sometimes it is," the wizard replied. "And sometimes I'm astonished that they don't hang the lot of us
and be done with it."

The thought that this terrible decision might by
governed by nothing but his own whim was even more

appalling than thinking destiny had led him here. "Then I'm not surprised you all become ghosts," Dayven retorted.

Reddick grinned. "The Cenzar don't believe in ghosts."

"The Cenzar are barbarians." But he didn't believe that, not anymore. When had his opinion of them changed? He hoped Vadeen had been found before he became too uncomfortable. But Vadeen's discomfort would only be physical—*his* path was clear. Dayven would gladly trade places with him. "I don't know," he said aloud. "I don't think I know anything anymore."

"In a wizard," said Reddick gently, "that's a good sign. The less you know, the more you ask."

It didn't feel good. "When do I get some answers?"

"No idea, kid. I haven't got 'em yet."

"Wonderful." A trickle of rain soaked through the blanket and rolled down Dayven's neck. He sneezed. It was better than crying.

The next two days' of riding were a misery of wet, cold, and mud. The nights were hard for different reasons.

A firm hand shook Dayven out of blood-soaked dreams. "No!" he shouted, flailing wildly. His fist struck something solid that caught and held it.

"Wake up," said Reddick soothingly. "You're dreaming."

"It was Soren." Dayven clung to his tutor, shaking. "He was fighting the Cenzar. He . . . I dreamed they . . ."

"Only a nightmare." Reddick patted his shoulder.

Dayven sat up abruptly and released Reddick's robe. "I'm sorry," he said coldly. "Did I wake you?"

"That's all right." Reddick returned to his own bedroll. "It must have been quite a dream though. You want to talk about it?"

"No," said Dayven. The silence lengthened. The last thing he wanted was to ask the wizard for help, but the need to know grew until he had to speak.

"Reddick, do wizards know about dreams?"

"You have 'em when you're asleep."

Dayven snorted. "But do wizard's dreams ever mean anything?"

"No more than anyone else's. Sometimes you dream about things that worry you. Sometimes dreams don't seem to mean anything at all."

"They don't come true then? Wizards' dreams?"

"Not wizards' dreams particularly. I've heard about dreams coming true, but I've never had it happen. Or known anyone it's happened to. I don't think you have to worry about that."

"I'm sure *you* wouldn't." Dayven rolled away from his tutor and waited, in open-eyed silence, for dawn.

The mud slowed them, but on the evening of the third day they saw the Town-within-the-Walls.

"We're at least two hours' ride out." Reddick squinted into the distance. "It wouldn't matter even if we made it; they're closing the gates. They wouldn't open them just to let wizards in. One more camp."

Dayven studied the familiar towers in the glowing light. His father had come to this city when he was only a boy, to be Watcherlad to the previous Lordowner. Dayven had been born within its walls. He remembered how much his mother had loved it.

"The Cenzar called it Miskafar. They built it, didn't they?" Now that he knew Cenzar stonework he could see their craft in every line and arch.

"Of course." Reddick had found some dry wood and was starting a fire. "That wasn't the work of three generations, more like ten."

Dayven sat down with a thump and held out his hands to the blaze. He realized that he had already made his decision, sometime on that miserable rainy ride. He just hadn't been willing to admit it, until now. He was cold, and so tired he almost didn't care anymore. Almost.

"Finally," said Reddick. "A different scowl."

"What?"

"Ever since you eavesdropped on our conference, you've been wearing the scowl of someone trying to make an impossible decision. Now you're wearing the scowl of someone who's made a decision, but doesn't like it."

Dayven's jaw dropped, but no sound came out.

"One thing, kid. If you've decided to tell Lord Enar our plan, give me a chance to warn the other wizards to get out. Will you do that?"

"You'd give me a chance to tell him?"

"How could I stop you?" Reddick asked calmly. "You think I could kill you?"

"No," said Dayven. "I know you won't." That mattered to him more than he cared to admit. "But I didn't think you sensed me on the roof. Didn't the spell work?"

"Oh, your spell was great; I didn't sense you at all. Vadeen on the other hand . . ."

"Oh." Dayven blushed.

"You'll learn. You've got real talent for magic. For

spying . . . Maybe with practice."

"Don't you get tired of living a lie all the time?" Dayven asked.

"You mean my reputation? I don't have to do it all the time. Only enough to maintain the image in public. And it isn't entirely a lie. I was pretty wild when I was younger. I started to outgrow it about the same time I realized how useful it could be."

"Why?"

Reddick's brows rose. "Surely you figured that out?"

"I meant, why did you outgrow it?"

"I became a wizard," said Reddick. "It's hard to waste your life once you've discovered the world is this beautiful."

The peace in his face had been the same the night he held fire in his hands.

Looking around the rain-drenched hill top, Dayven saw the subtle colors of the long grass. A spider busily mended a torn web. Some small animal had left tracks in the mud. He felt as if he had never seen any of these things before and they would always be new. This was what it was to be a wizard. A lump rose in his throat.

"So." Reddick's voice seemed very far away. "What have you decided?"

"I'm going to help you," said Dayven. "I'll tell Lord

Enar whatever you want."

"I'm glad. When you're a wizard, you'll—"

"No," said Dayven. "I'm going to be a Guardian. I made a vow to my mother. It's what I always wanted."

"What you wanted? Or did you want it because she wanted it?"

Dayven's face hardened. "I have worked no trick of magic that has altered the destiny of any man. My decision is made. I won't change it."

"Let me understand this. You want to be a Tharn Guardian, but you're going to side with the wizards and betray the Tharn?"

"That has nothing to do with it," said Dayven. "Not really. Sooner or later the Tharn . . . *we* will leave this land. If we leave now, the land and its people will live. And probably fewer will die in open battle than if we all starve in a siege. This valley belongs to the Cenzar, no matter what that old prophecy said. It always has. Better to return it now, alive, and live ourselves."

"It's not really that simple. You're right, as far as it goes, but for the Tharn the fighting won't end when they leave. There are other tribes in the forest now. Wherever they go, they'll have to fight to make room for themselves."

"But if we win this battle and the valley dies we'll

have to move on and fight anyway. And the Cenzar farmers will be forced to move, and fight for land, as well."

"You got it, kid. It wasn't simple, but you saw all the sides. I'm proud of you."

"What will happen to the wizards when the Tharn go?"

Reddick shrugged. "If they don't throw us out, we'll probably go with them. Or maybe stay with the Cenzar. Maybe both. Wizards move around a lot. It will be hard for the Tharn, for a while."

"I'll be with them," said Dayven.

"Ah, I'm beginning to understand. You're going to betray your people, but you're going to renounce magic to punish yourself. Am I right?"

If he was, Dayven wasn't about to tell him so. "To keep what I can of my oaths, to my mother and Soren, is the only shred of honor I'll have left!" His last hope of holding on to his true destiny.

"You don't think keeping this valley alive is honorable?"

"I'm not sure what's honorable anymore," said Dayven. "The creed doesn't cover this. But I think it's the right thing to do."

"Honor isn't the same as right?'

"My mother said honor was loyalty to your people."

"Doesn't that definition seem a little narrow?"

"My mother was a good woman! My grandmother brought dishonor—"

"Your mother wasn't a wizard. And you should be."

"*Should be?* Nothing is the way it should be! If she knew what I was doing now, she would hate me! Soren is going to fight in that battle. He might get hurt. He might—" Dayven's voice broke and he turned away.

Reddick sighed. "It's your choice."

"Don't worry. I've made it." Dayven rubbed his eyes. "If you persuade Lord Enar to fight the Cenzar on the plain, instead of trying to withstand a siege, are you sure the Cenzar will win?"

"No." Reddick shook his head. "The armies are just about evenly matched. That's why we're going to cast weakening spells on the Tharn equipment. Straps will break, bowstrings will snap, spears will fly off balance, that kind of thing. You want to learn a spell to make armor come apart?"

"No." Dayven's mouth was tight. "I want you to teach me a spell to prevent it."

CHAPTER TWELVE

THEY ENTERED THE CITY that morning, and Dayven found himself in the Lorcowner's presence before noon. It was much the same as the last time: the big man, towering in his chair, the carved oak staff at his side. And like the last time, there were no witnesses except Soren and Lore Master Senna.

It was only in Dayven's imagination that his Grandmother Adina's spirit stood beside him, offering support—trying to help him calm his pounding heart.

"Did you have any trouble getting away from the wizard to come here?" Lord Enar asked.

"No, Lord," said Dayven. "Reddick knows that Soren is my best friend—the closest member of my family still alive. For me to visit him at once seemed natural." His throat ached with the truth of it. He was betraying Soren as well, but what other choice did he have? Obedience to the Lordowner was the second rule, but defending the weak was the first. And that was what the wizards were doing, wasn't it?

"Good," said Lord Enar. "Tell us what you've learned."

Lore Master Senna moved, with his slow limping pace, to a bench by the wall. Dayven couldn't look at him without turning away from the Lordowner, but he could feel the old bard's cold, watchful gaze. He drew a deep, steadying breath and launched his tale.

He began with a truthful account of his journey to Damishaff, of the dammed river, and how Reddick had freed the captured peasants. He knew that the Tharn troop captain would already have reported that incident. And if he left out the wondrous joy of his first experiences with magic, well, that wasn't a lie . . .

Describing what had happened in Damishaff was harder.

"So you stayed in this zondar," said Lord Enar. "How well could you keep track of Reddick's doings while you were there?"

"Not as well as before," Dayven acknowledged. "I spent most mornings working with the Cenzar teachers, and I learned some things about the way they fight—especially about the way they use horses in battle—that I should tell the Sword Master."

"Really?" asked Lord Enar, diverted. "It's been a long time since we fought a serious battle with the Cenzar. The bards' accounts talk about their fighting techniques, and some of the older Guardians remember them, but no one has seen them fight recently."

"I'd be happy to pass that information on," said Dayven. "In fact, Reddick suggested that I should." To avert suspicion from the both of them, the wizard said. Was he betraying Vadeen now? What a twisted path this was—surely not a true one.

"But that's a matter for later," Lore Master Senna reminded them both smoothly. "When you were learning these things, you couldn't have been watching the wizard."

"No, sir," said Dayven. "He spent most of his time in Damishaff talking with his friends in the zondar, but there were times he went out into the city, and I don't know who he met or what he did then."

Still truth, still within the technical definition of honor. But the lie, the monstrous betrayal, was almost upon him. Could he do it? Could he really betray his

155

Lord, his cousin, and his people? Dayven summoned up the memory of the scrawny crops, the wasted, sickly fields, and spread it over his heart like a shield.

Soren cleared his throat, nervous at speaking out in such high company. "They were in the Cenzar city less than a week. Could the wizard, could anyone, plot treason in such a short time? A handful of meetings?"

Lord Enar met the Lore Master's eyes. Dayven couldn't tell what he read there.

"There's no way to know, is there?" said Lord Enar slowly. "No way to be absolutely sure. So I suppose the real question is: Do you trust this wizard?"

"Yes, Lord," said Dayven. "I trust him."

The truth of it rang in his voice for all to hear. Lord Enar settled back in his chair, his shoulders relaxing in satisfaction, and even the Lore Master nodded.

So truth created the ultimate lie. Was this what the world was like for wizards? This thorny, gray tangle where right and wrong were so mixed there was no telling them apart?

Dayven stood straight, watching the man to whom he owed loyalty with calm eyes. Only his heart wept.

Dayven ran his hands over the strap that fastened Soren's breastplate as he helped him into it.

"You could have fought beside us," said Soren. "Since the wizards aren't planning treachery, there's no reason to go on pretending you're going to be one."

Lord Enar had offered to make him a Guardian in time for the battle, in return for his services, but the Lore Master had protested against it, claiming that they shouldn't reveal anything to the wizards till after the battle was over. Dayven hadn't objected—he could do all he needed serving as Soren's Watcherlad.

The morning wind blowing over the great plain rattled the canvas of Soren's tent. The others had thought Soren mad to ask a wizard's apprentice to help him arm for his first battle.

"I'm out of practice," said Dayven shortly. Soren's loyalty would have had him in tears, but tears would have interfered with what he was doing. He ran his hands over the next piece of armor, checking for spells of weakening.

"You spent most of last week practicing with the Cenzar," Soren pointed out. "Dayven, what's wrong?"

"Nothing," said Dayven.

He fought down the memory of Lord Enar's voice: *I suppose the real question is: Do you trust this wizard?*

He had spoken nothing but the truth. *I'm sorry, Lord,* he told Lord Enar now, in the depths of his own mind.

But you asked the wrong question. You should have asked: Can you trust me?

"Dayven!" Soren yanked his shield from his cousin's absent grasp.

A trumpet blew. Soren's head lifted toward it, then he looked back at his cousin. "There's something you're not telling me. You've been avoiding me since you came back. What's wrong?"

"That's the first call," said Dayven. "We'd better get your horse." He had checked the bridle by the time his cousin caught up with him, and started on the girths.

"Dayven, you haven't altered anyone's destiny with magic, have you? Fallen for some wizard's trickery?"

"No." Dayven's heart twisted. "I have altered no one's destiny . . . by magic."

"Then what is it?"

Dayven began checking the horse's hooves. As his fingers touched the shoe on the right forehoof, he felt the familiar tingling. The trumpet sounded again.

"Curse it," Soren swore. "I have to go."

"Get your helmet," said Dayven. "I'll bring the horse in a minute."

As Soren raced back to the tent, Dayven's mind touched the spell of weakness that tainted the nails holding the shoe. They would break as soon as the horse began to gallop. At best the beast would become lame as the day wore on. At worst he might stumble, throwing his rider under the pounding hooves. Dayven banished the fragile spell and placed his own will on the nails, that they stay whole and strong and hold the shoe as they were made to. Imposing your will on inanimate objects, Reddick had called it. For a moment Dayven thought about the other knights, those who would fall victim to the wizards' treachery But the Tharn had to lose this battle—and that meant some of them would die. He dropped the hoof and looked up. Soren was staring at him. The trumpet called for the last time. "When this is over," Soren took the reins and swung into the saddle, "we're going to have a long talk, cousin."

Dayven stared after his friend until he could no longer see him. Would Soren ever understand that it was wizards' truths, not wizards' trickery, that had changed him? Would his cousin even survive this battle, and have the chance to try? No answer came. Dayven turned and made his way to the surgeons' tent.

The wizards arrived as a group, about an hour before the battle began. Male and female, plump and thin, shabby and well-groomed—the only thing they had in common was the gray of their robes, and the calm determination with which they met the surgeons' scowls. Wizards' healing might not be respectable, but no sane man, faced with the choice between magic and amputation, would refuse their aid.

Dayven spent the day of the battle tripping over things that were in plain sight. All the healers, both wizards and surgeons, cursed his clumsiness and finally set him to the simplest task available—stirring a great pot of brewing herbs for poultices. The herbs stank, but Dayven didn't object. With his hands on the stirring stick, he was free to keep his mind on visions of Soren.

He watched his cousin waiting for the order to charge, late-morning sun beating on the helmet that concealed Soren's face, his lance easy in hand.

He saw the battle begin, his cousin in the front line, sweeping down on the Cenzar.

He saw the moment that the well-aimed lance pierced a Cenzar body, and how Soren, ignoring the chaos raging around him, stopped his horse and stared down at the first man he had killed.

A healer shook him, cursing. "I said add another packet of arrowroot! Are you deaf?" He hurried off. Dayven found the packet and fumbled blindly, tearing it and dumping the contents into the pot.

160

He saw Soren, ahead of his men, surrounded by Cenzar. On their swift horses, the Cenzar warriors swarmed and darted like bees. One of their blades flicked under Soren's helmet and a trickle of red crept down his breastplate before his men reached him. Soren never stopped fighting.

Dayven watched his cousin, as the sun was setting, fall back from the battle to rest his weary horse. His sword was reddened the length of the blade, his leather gauntlets soaked with blood. Soren reached up and pulled off his helmet.

Dayven saw his cousin's face, already changed, change again as he looked over the battlefield and realized that the Tharn were going to lose.

Tears began to creep down Dayven's cheeks, but Soren's expression only hardened. Safe behind the lines, Dayven watched his cousin replace his helmet and return to the battle, risking his life for a cause already lost.

It was night.

Sounds of celebration from the Cenzar camp drifted into the surgeons' tent, mingling with the moans of the wounded. Dayven hated the Cenzar.

He hated Lord Enar, who was in the Cenzar camp, agreeing to leave the valley with all his people in exchange for his life and the lives of his men.

161

He hated the wizards as they moved among the worst of the wounded in the guttering torchlight. Their power flowed prodigally, altering men's destinies by saving their lives. It caressed Dayven's skin like a living creature.

He hated Lore Master Senna, who claimed he had come to help the healers, but who spent most of his time watching the wizards—his own anger and shame naked on his usually unreadable face.

But most of all—as the Tharn soldiers cursed the black fate that had seemed to dog their every step—with an aching, bitterness, Dayven hated himself.

As he moved among the wounded with water and bandages, the small glow of his power was the only brightness in the gloom that seemed to wrap the Tharn camp. Dayven did nothing that could be observed by the sharp-eyed Lore Master, by anyone who wasn't a wizard, but blood flowed slower from wounds he bandaged, and men who moaned and tossed in anguish fell peacefully asleep soon after he wiped their sweating foreheads. Even in the midst of his own depression, the use of his magic to heal and ease was unspeakably sweet. As a Guardian, he would vow never to use magic again.

Soren's troop came into the tent, bearing more

stretchers. The Guardians' creed said that all the wounded, enemy and friend, were to be carried from the field and cared for equally, but no troop except Soren's was carrying the Cenzar wounded in. And the surgeons were very slow to tend them.

Soren was the only person Dayven didn't hate.

His one wound was a shallow cut at the base of his throat. Watching his cousin now, as he gently set down the foot of the stretcher he carried, Dayven felt a rush of gratitude. That, at least, he had done right.

"Hey, surgeon!" Soren's voice was hoarse with shouting. "I've got a bad one here."

One of the surgeons went to him. The wizard Sundar finished a healing spell and followed. Dayven gave his water jug to another apprentice and went to help.

"It'll have to come off," said the surgeon grimly, leaning over the terrible wound. "He took a sword right through the knee. The joint is shattered."

"I can mend it." Sundar stepped forward. "I still have enough power."

The surgeon stood and faced him. Dayven's eyes left the smashed joint and found the wounded man's face.

It was Vadeen.

Dayven's heart throbbed, and then began to pound,

163

sickly. He had almost forgotten he had *two* friends in this battle. How could he have forgotten?

"If you're going to use magic, wizard, it'll be for one of our own kind," the surgeon said.

Vadeen was unconscious, his usually mobile face gray and slack, his eyes ringed with shadows.

"He'll probably die if you amputate," Sundar argued. "As a surgeon, aren't you sworn to heal everyone you can?"

A one-legged man would ride in no great races. A one-legged man could not be a rashief.

"Not by letting people work magic on them, I'm not." The surgeon extended his arms to block Sundar's path.

I am not here. It was harder, in a well-lit room, full of people, but he could do it. *I am not here. An apprentice with a tray of bandages in the surgeon's tent. What could be less noticeable? No one can notice me. Your eyes will drift over me. I am like a chair or a cot, a part of this place. I am not here.*

Dayven slipped behind the surgeon's back and knelt beside Vadeen. The sword had cut deep into his knee, severing bone and muscle. Dayven laid his hands on the wound and let all the power he had suppressed and concealed surge through them.

His eyes closed.

He felt the shattered bones begin to move together, the torn ligaments reaching for each other, the veins knitting to bring blood to damaged muscle. Finally, he let the power ebb and felt the weariness of his own body. Then he heard the odd pocket of silence that surrounded him, and knew what it meant. It took all the courage he possessed to open his eyes.

His hands were dyed with blood, but the joint beneath them was whole. Vadeen would wake, and find that the life he had chosen still lay before him. That was worth the price, wasn't it? Dayven lifted his head.

They were all staring at him, the surgeons, the wounded, the wizard. Lore Master Senna simply nodded, as if something he'd known all along had finally been confirmed. It was in Soren's horrified gaze that Dayven read the irrevocability of what he had done. The chain of destiny seized him, stifling, inescapable.

Dayven sprang to his feet and ran.

The sun was rising when Reddick found him, sitting on the edge of a meadow far from the battlefield, staring at his cupped hands.

The wizard carried a gray robe, folded neatly over one arm—the symbol of a test that Dayven had passed. A test he hadn't even been aware of.

Reddick sat beside Dayven and let the silence grow until, when he spoke, his voice did not interrupt the peace around them. Odd that someone so boisterous possessed so much peace.

"They sent Vadeen back to the Cenzar camp. He wanted to send you a message, but they wouldn't let him talk to me. And Soren wouldn't speak to him."

"I've lost Soren." A butterfly crawled out of Dayven's cupped hands and on to the base of his thumb, flexing new wings in the sunlight. He let fall the scraps of the sundered cocoon. He'd lost Soren, and his honor, and his home. But what had he found?

"Maybe," said Reddick. "People surprise you sometimes. Of course, sometimes they don't. You saved Vadeen. Do you care more for Soren than for him?"

Dayven's eyes were on the butterfly.

"I loved . . . I love both of them." Yes, that was what he'd found. And life, and magic—his true path.

The butterfly lifted and darted away in the golden light.

"It really isn't simple, is it Dayven?"

"No," said Dayven. "But it's the way it should be."